# The Proxy Bride

# The Proxy Bride

Terri Favro

QUATTRO BOOKS

The publication of *The Proxy Bride* has been generously supported by the Canada Council for the Arts and the Ontario Arts Council.

 Canada Council for the Arts  Conseil des Arts du Canada   ONTARIO ARTS COUNCIL CONSEIL DES ARTS DE L'ONTARIO

Author's photograph: Ayelet Tsabari
Cover image: Terri Favro
Cover design: Diane Mascherin
Editor: Luciano Iacobelli
Typography: Grey Wolf Typography

Library and Archives Canada Cataloguing in Publication

Favro, Terri
        The proxy bride / Terri Favro.

Issued also in an electronic format.

ISBN 978-1-927443-06-4

        I. Title.

PS8611.A93P76 2012        C813'.6        C2012-903890-3

Published by Quattro Books Inc.
382 College Street
Toronto, Ontario, M5T 1S8
www.quattrobooks.ca

Printed in Canada

*For Ron*

*The real hero is always a hero by mistake;*
*he dreams of being an honest coward like everybody else.*

*– Umberto Eco*

# 1

*June 20, 1969*
*Shipman's Corners, Ontario*

THE RED-AND-BLUE-striped AEROPOSTE envelope arrives not long after Marcello unlocks the front of the store. He can see the postman working his way, door by door, along Canal Road. Across the street at Kowalchuck Flowers, a few foundry and slaughterhouse workers, up all night at craps, lounge on the front stoop drinking coffee and playing *rock, paper, scissors* to rouse themselves enough to survive the morning shift. Their foreman, Stinky, raises a cup, saluting Marcello with his one good arm: a friendly reminder of the twenty bucks he's still owed from the game two nights ago. Marcello nods back, the new debt still fresh and painful. Despite a quick prayer to St. Anthony of Padua every time he rolled the dice, Marcello lost, and lost, and lost. As usual.

Opening the sweet shop is supposed to be his father's job but Senior has fallen asleep in front of the television again; Marcello can hear the buzz of the test pattern. The way he's going, Pop is sure to blow the picture tube. Marcello walks into the storeroom, turns off the overheating TV, and tries to shake his father awake.

"*Pronto*," Senior grunts, rolling over on the cot. As Marcello tugs the blanket up over his father's hunched shoulder, his foot hits an empty Hiram Walker bottle, sending it rolling across the floor into a wadded up copy of *Oggi*. A laughing Gina Lollabrigida gazes up at him, her lovely face a stained and wrinkled mess. Marcello frowns: Pop is usually more careful with the gossip papers, neatly refolding them for paying customers after he's finished with them. He doesn't want to think about what his father has been up to with this copy.

*Beh.* Just another beautiful morning at Italian Tobacco & Sweets.

He drops the ruined *Oggi* into the trash bin, stuffs a rolled-up *Popular Science* into the back of his jeans, and takes his breakfast of instant coffee and Nutella on white bread out into the sunshine on the front stoop. With his nose in the magazine, he can ignore the assholes across the street. He flips to an article called "Generation Moon," sips his Nescafé and reads:

*By 1980, the Sea of Tranquility will be home to a teeming lunar metropolis, complete with apartment houses, schools, hospitals, hydroponic farms, and places of worship, all under geodesic domes powered by solar energy.*

'Places of worship' – like churches, thinks Marcello. A Catholic president launched the space program. It stands to reason that not long after Apollo 11 lands, NASA will start sending settlers into space, priests among them. Life as an astronaut-priest might make even celibacy bearable.

In the fall, Marcello will be off to the seminary – that is, if he can win back the money he lost to Stinky for his novitiate fee. But with three months to go, there's still plenty of time to hit a winning streak. Bound to happen, sooner or later.

Next door, Christie Hryhorchuck, lanky and beautiful in her kilt and white blouse, lets herself out of her house to go to school. She blows a kiss to Marcello that he's just about to return when the postman appears.

"Looks like something from the old country," he says, handing Marcello the envelope. "Hope nobody passed away."

Marcello laughs. "You kidding me? All they do in Italy is die and send us snapshots of the funerals to cheer us up."

The postman chuckles and pats Marcello's back.

He can feel the weight of the photograph in the envelope; probably a black-and-white glossy of yet another ancient relative nestled in a shroud. The translucently thin airmail paper is addressed to *Trovato, Marcello, 10 Via Canale, Shipmans Corners, Ontario, CANADA.*

Reluctantly, Marcello leaves the sunshine to go back into the shop. "Letter for you, Pop," he calls, flipping it onto the counter between the dusty box of two-for-a-penny caramels and the grubby bag of licorice cigars.

Senior shuffles out of the storeroom. He's still in his bathrobe but has managed to wash his face and slick his hair straight back from a forehead as deeply furrowed as the fields bordering Canal Road. He picks up the envelope without looking at his son, returns to the storeroom and slams the door. A fug of body odour follows him.

*How did I ever come out of* you? wonders Marcello, eyeing the disappearing wreck of his father. The television seems to have swallowed him whole.

Like just about everything they own, the TV is second-hand; Marcello found it at the curb in front of the Donato house a couple of weeks earlier. It was a Westinghouse, a good make. He squatted down to inspect the set but could see nothing wrong with it. Finally, he decided to knock on the door.

Claudia Donato answered in slippers, housedress and apron, a kerchief knotted over her lacquered dome of black hair, a cigarette drooping between two fingers, bright orange nails filed to lethal points.

He gave a respectful nod. "Sorry to bother you, Missus. Just wanted to ask about that TV on your curb."

Claudia squinted past him into the street, then refocused on his face. "Thought you was one of those damn Jehovah's Witnesses. Or the Fuller Brush guy again." Softly, she added: "You from Kowalchuck's Flowers? I thought he said, tomorrow. I just done my nails." She shook a hand in the air, the tips of her fingers tiny creamsicle daggers.

Marcello tried to make sense of all this. "I'm from nowhere, Missus. I was just walking along, and saw the set, and wondered if it was up for grabs." Truthful to a fault, he added: "I work for Kowalchuck sometimes, though."

Claudia took a long drag on her cigarette, shading her eyes from the sun. "Okay, I get it. Thought you'd be older, is all. You look like an overgrown kid."

A bit hurt by the *overgrown*, Marcello said: "I'm nineteen, Missus Donato."

"Don't call me 'Missus'. Makes me sound like a *nonna*. I'm only thirty-four. Call me 'Claudia'."

"Claudia, then," said Marcello, uncomfortable calling an adult woman by her first name. "That TV – is the picture tube okay?"

She exhaled a thin stream of smoke and gave an indifferent shrug: "Far as I know."

"So why're you throwing it out?" he asked, hoping she'd say – *just take it, for Christ's sake.* Instead she tossed her half-smoked cigarette at Marcello's sneakers and swung the door open for him: "We got a new RCA colour console, that's why. See for yourself." Wishing he had just taken the set without asking, he stepped inside.

The interior of the house was in shadow, the windows covered by thick sheers and Roman shades. In the gloom of the living room, Claudia gestured for him to make himself comfortable on the plastic-covered brocade couch. Without a cigarette, she didn't seem to know what to do with her hands: she blew on her nails and fiddled with the hi-fi, until finally she unknotted her kerchief and apron and tossed them onto a chair.

"Lemme put some music on and we can get this the hell over with," she sighed.

In the time it took Jack Jones to sing "Wives and Lovers," Claudia relieved Marcello of his tee shirt, jeans, underwear, and virginity. Everything happened so fast that when he thought about it later, all he could remember was a waterfall of still images, like the postcard packs of panoramic views of Niagara Falls they sold in a rack at the candy store: his briefs puddled under a glass end table covered with china figurines of dancing shepherdesses; his thighs, thick with black hair, pressed against the plastic couch cover, as Missus Donato (*Claudia, for Christ's sake!*) rolled a condom down his awestruck penis and straddled him, her puckered brown nipples dancing on his lips, her nails gouging tangerine trails into the skin of his chest. All against a soundtrack of her hoarse little grunts and the lush voice on the stereo singing *Hey little girl comb your hair fix your makeup.* After crying out in a voice he didn't recognize, he was almost immediately ready to do it again but

Claudia was up and off him in a flash, ordering, "Get dressed, Al gets off shift early sometimes and the twins are due home any minute now from drum majorette practice."

As he reached under the glass table for his briefs, Marcello – having just done it for the first time, with a woman who, if not quite old enough to be his mother, could certainly have been his big sister – struggled to find the right words to mark the occasion. He settled on: "Was I okay?"

Crouched on the floor as she wiped the plastic couch cover with her panties, Claudia squinted up at him: "What? Why do you care?"

He hesitated, then confessed: "Because I'm not the guy you were expecting."

"Not the guy?" Claudia stood up, her brows forming a long, dark line like storm clouds on the horizon. "I know you now. The twins talk about you. You're the candy man's son. The one who's gonna be a priest, right?"

Marcello nodded.

"*Non fa niente*, Lollipop. We'll call it even trade, so long as you do something for me." She jabbed an orange-tipped finger in his face: "Tell Kowalchuck what we just done. Tell him that that as far as I'm concerned, our debt is settled. He has to leave us alone, now – me, Al and the twins. *Especially* the twins. If another guy turns up at my door tomorrow looking for a freebie, he'll get it slammed in his fucking face." Claudia started rubbing her eyes, as if trying to push back tears: "Damn contact lenses."

Despite the unladylike language and smudges of black mascara and orange nail lacquer all over her face, Marcello thought Claudia as glamourous as Elizabeth Taylor. He wished he had something to give her. Having nothing else to offer, he gave her his word.

"Claudia," he said, gently. "I promise I'll tell Kowalchuck to leave you alone. First chance I get. If he'll listen to me. But in the meantime, can I take the TV?"

She got shakily to her feet and made a feral sound, a cross between a sob and a growl, as she caught sight of something:

"Oh Jesus. Oh shit shit shit." It was the condom, lying empty on the rug.

Accusingly, she picked it up and handed it to Marcello. It looked like a long white leech that had shriveled in the sun.

"Must have fallen off," he admitted. "Never used one before."

Claudia put her hands over her face. Her manicure was a mess. "Get out of here. And take the goddamn Westinghouse with you."

He dressed rapidly, in silence – underwear, shirt, jeans, sneakers, like a movie running backward. By the time he stepped back into the sunshine of the front stoop, no more than twenty minutes had passed since he'd knocked to ask about the TV.

As Marcello lugged the set home, cradled in his arms like a baby, the pressure of the load caused a pleasantly painful sensation against the crosshatch of orange lacquered scratches on his chest. Stung like hell but he found himself saying a blasphemous prayer that they would never heal, that they would just keep bleeding as a lasting physical reminder of ecstasy.

He would have to confess this sin, eventually, although right now, he wasn't sorry: everyone had to do it some time, and at least he got it out of his system before taking a vow of celibacy. God the Father Himself was a guy; Marcello was pretty sure He'd understand.

Passing Senior at the counter, he said, "I got us a TV today, Pop."

Senior followed his son into the storeroom and watched as he hooked up the set and adjusted the rabbit ears.

"What it cost you?"

"Not much. A little sweat. Now we can watch *ABC Wide World of Sports*. The thrill of victory, the agony of...."

"*They don't have sports in this country*," Senior interrupted in Italian. "*No soccer. Only hockey, and baseball from l'America.*"

Clicking the dial, all they could find was channel after channel of women in luxurious living rooms, weeping in front of handsome men in suits. Everyone was drinking tumblers of Scotch in the middle of the day.

"Soap operas," sighed Marcello. "I guess that's all that's on TV in the afternoon."

Senior sat down on the army cot and watched with interest; the show was called *Secret Storm*. After it finished, there was a station break and another show began with a deep voice saying: *Like sand through the hourglass, so go the days of our lives.* Marcello reached out to change the channel.

"Leave it," said Senior, catching his son's arm.

Ever since then, Marcello has been marooned at the candy counter, listening to the tears and accusations, infidelities and love affairs, cases of amnesia and mistaken identity leaking through the storeroom door.

Just yesterday, Marcello went in for a box of candy cigarettes and found his father slumped on an army cot, weeping, his thick hands spread over his face. Marcello knelt down next to him, genuinely concerned. "What's the matter, Pop? You sick or something?"

"It's Denise! Her husband has been stolen away by that rich *puttana*, Serena."

"You're crying over a soap opera? These people aren't real, Pop!"

Senior wiped his face with the back of his hand. "*You have no passion in your soul,*" he told his son fiercely in Italian. "*You've lived in this cold country so long, you can't feel anything anymore. At least in my stories, people really live!*"

The only thing that gets Senior away from the TV is the arrival of 'special customers', guys who turn up at all hours, asking for what's under the counter in the detergent box printed with the words *Cheer! THIS END UP.*

The magazines come from many different lands but the girls on the covers are interchangeable: she's always a blonde with her head thrown back, red lips parted, half-closed eyelids painted ice blue. Sometimes she squeezes her enormous breasts, the red talons of her fingernails pinching erect nipples.

The magazines started as a sideline but quickly became bigger moneymakers than wax lips and creamsicles. Now sailors from the canal boats come to the candy store when their ships dock to take on supplies. Neighbourhood men drop in after Sunday mass to pick up some smokes and a little reading material. Some nights, the craps players show up with their winnings, wanting a woman from the back of the pool hall but ready to settle for one of Senior's glossy paper whores. As Stinky once pointed out to Marcello, crouched in the alley behind Kowalchuck's Flower Shop: *Your Pop's girlies don't try to cheat you and they won't give you the clap.*

Like the DPs who climbed out of the wreckage of postwar Europe to settle on Canal Road, the Cheer girls are stateless and many-tongued: *We got 'em in Italian, Polish, Yugoslavian, German, Russian and Dutch, brought in special from over-the-river,* Senior tells his customers proudly. *Hard core, the way Europeans like it, not that arty American 'Playboy' crap.* But he is careful who he brags to; smuggling obscene material across the Niagara River could land both Marcello Senior and Junior in jail. But they've never been caught, not once, because Kowalchuck – a successful businessman – runs the show.

"No shitboxes! Shitboxes are a dead giveaway!" Kowalchuck warned when Senior tried to smuggle the magazines inside Marcello Junior's '53 Chevy, a salvaged demolition derby car. Instead, the goods are hidden inside a gleaming white 1966 Impala registered in Niagara Glen's elderly mother's name, a sticker affixed to the bumper from a tourist attraction in upstate Pennsylvania called *Holyland USA.*

From time to time, Kowalchuck polishes the chassis to a sheen with Turtle Wax and crosses the Rainbow Bridge to Niagara Falls, New York, and back, with old Mrs. K. in the passenger seat, a box of Bibles in her lap bearing the imprint of a conservative Buffalo priest whose Latin masses are televised on both sides of the border. Mrs. K. religiously declares the full purchase price of the Bibles to the boys at

Canada Customs who see the little-old-lady car so often that they wave it through without a second look. Which, of course, is the point. Sometimes the magazines are slipped under the Bibles (*simple plans work best*, preaches Kowalchuck) but the Impala is a honeycomb of hiding places, the most salacious ladies rolled and stuffed inside the rocker panels, twelve at a time – *Like the Apostles*, as Senior points out. For those few guards smart enough to notice something fishy about the white car, Kowalchuck invests some of the venture's profits in a little wheel greasing.

Marcello Junior's job is easy: he provides what Kowalchuck refers to as muscle. He's the one to pry off and replace the rocker panels on the Impala, to stack and carry boxes carefully hidden in the storeroom under licorice pipes and mojos, and most importantly to deal with any guys who arrive at the store drunk and horny, expecting a free sample. Kowalchuck has provided him with a simple, cheap, easy-to-use weapon, a baseball bat, which so far he's never had to swing at anyone. When the occasional craps player staggers in without sufficient cash, Marcello simply stands at the counter tapping the bat in his hand, making himself look big. Not difficult, at six-four. While he proves to be effective at intimidation, he's never actually had to lay a hand on anyone – a good thing, since along with gambling and the as-yet-unconfessed carnal knowledge of Claudia Donato, physical violence would be another thing to bring up to his confessor, another sin to live down, or work off, or repent before he enters the seminary. For now, the money he makes safeguarding the store's print merchandise is a means to an end: that's how Marcello sees it, the goal being saving up for his novitiate fee so he can get the hell out of Shipman's Corners.

Marcello may have Senior's tall, powerful build but everything else about him – his thickly-lashed eyes, curly hair, and sensuous mouth like a *putto* – must come from his shadowy mother. Not that he knows for sure, having never seen a picture of her. But a few broken images scratch at his memory: a woman's hands briskly adjusting the ties of an apron; wet footprints next to his on a bare cement floor; a bready, warm presence beside him on the deck of a ship, the blue horizon rising and falling, falling and rising. His first solid, too-real-not-to-be-true memory of Canada is of himself holding Sofia's hand in a train station, staring up at words, high as stars, chiselled in stone. A friendly man with a spectacular mustache walked them to a platform: *Signore IIAS*, Sofia called him. Mister Italian Immigrant Aid Society. He presented a sucker to Marcello and mussed his hair, saying *Hey, paesano, you already got it made, your Pop owns a candy store!*

Marcello and his mother were part of a pattern repeated again and again on Canal Road: men arrived first, settled themselves, then sent for their families. They had only just joined Senior when an outbreak of infantile paralysis, also known as poliomyelitis, swept Shipman's Corners. Polio was something you worried about with children but it bypassed Marcello and attacked Sofia. The doctor who came to the flat suggested that the stress of looking after the boy on the long journey might have predisposed her to the illness. Marcello can still remember Senior repeating these words in Italian, and looking down at him accusingly.

She was rushed to the hospital and confined to an iron lung. To Marcello, her absence was a hole in time, a void that cuddled in bed beside him, chilly lips chanting words against his skin:

> *Say the rosary and she'll come home.*
> *Obey your father and she'll come home.*
> *Do as you're told and she'll come home.*
> *Be a good little boy or she'll die.*

Despite Marcello's attempts to bargain with God, Sofia died on Dominion Day, 1955. He was five years old. Kneeling at a coffin that seemed to hold a giant doll, he was overwhelmed by a childishly simple explanation for his mother's death:

> *Sono stato cattivo. E culpa mia.*
> *I was bad. It's my fault.*

Sofia vanished from his life like a rock dropped into a silent pool. Marcello's only memento of her is the record player she brought with her across the ocean, as if music didn't exist in Canada. Occasionally, at night, he heard it sing to him in his mother's voice; eventually even that comfort trickled away, leaving him with the lingering sense that anyone he loves, and who dares to love him back, is doomed to die. It is the act of loving that kills them, as if love carries with it a kind of temptation, or pride, that God won't tolerate. Real love is something you can only give to God. The punishment for loving someone other than God is to lose them to death. Marcello quietly believes this, something he has seen borne out several times in the passing of farm dogs.

As everyone knows, a father can't raise a child alone, especially one with a business to run. After a few too many trips to the hospital, where cuts from repeated slaps and punches from his grieving, grey-haired father were stitched and restitched, Marcello was sent to live with *paesani* of Senior's, the Andolini family: not exactly close relatives, but something more than friends. They came from the same part of war-torn Italy as Senior, with the same untranslatable jokes and ridiculously operatic tales of grand passion, lost love, terrible betrayals and sudden death – all from back in the Old Country, of course; no one lived or loved with such heat in polite, law-abiding Canada.

At the Andolini farm, Marcello was just one of many shouting, dark-haired boys, falling out of peach trees and fixing broken-down cars. There were so many kids that the Andolinis would hardly have even noticed Marcello, if not for his unusual height and odd interest in school. When he skipped a grade, one of the Andolini men observed: *the trouble with Marcello is that he thinks too much.*

He visited his Pop once a month; the family matriarch, Prima, saw to that. He remembers those grim visits, stuck indoors with his father, poking at the bags of jujubes and peppermints and playing with the door of the freezer where expensive treats sat unbought, month after month, until they were covered with frost. "Hey, knock it off!" Senior would yell. "You'll melt the goods!" Growing up, that was the longest conversation Marcello ever had with his father. If you can call it a conversation.

On his sixteenth birthday, Marcello was told to pack up and go home: Senior had wrenched his back lifting a box of Cee Dee Rockets and needed a hand in the store. Prima figured the boy was strong enough to both pull his weight and stand up to his father. *My conscience is clean,* she said. *Who's gonna push around a kid that big?*

He drove himself home to Shipman's Corners in his battered Chevy, carrying a few prized possessions: his mother's record player and 78s; a hockey stick signed by Stan Mikita; and a framed photograph of Pope John XXIII – a gift from Prima, who was the first to encourage Marcello's calling. *Every family should give one child to the Church,* she liked to say. One child, who would sacrifice himself to a life of celibacy and duty and love of God. As far as the Andolinis were concerned, Marcello was that child. It was the least the boy could do to thank the family for taking him in after his poor mother died.

Now, with just a couple of months to go before he enters the Passionate Order of St. John Seminary across the lake in Toronto, Marcello is starting to feel as if the muggy, tedious Niagara summer will go on forever – until that day when the letter arrives from Italy and Senior shuffles back out of the storeroom, holding a sheet of airmail paper and two snapshots. He takes his son by the arm and does something he almost never does: he smiles. "I have something important to show you."

Senior places the snapshots on the counter. The first is of a short blonde woman in a lace veil and a wedding dress as stiff as meringue. The neckline sags a little, as if the bodice is too big for her. In one hand, she grips a trailing bouquet of roses and freesia; the other is tucked into the arm of a grey-haired man in a pinstriped suit – too old to be the groom,

Marcello assumes he's her father. Like the bride, he looks like he's wearing someone else's clothes. The suit jacket strains over his belly and the cuffs of his pants almost cover his shoes. The man is smiling. The bride is not.

The second snapshot is a close-up of the same woman, taken at a table in what looks like an outdoor café. Her hair is scraped into a bun, showing off her huge blue eyes and delicate face, pale as a church angel. She smiles fetchingly, head tipped to one side, lips slightly parted. The pose looks disturbingly like that of a Cheer girl. Senior taps the woman's face with his finger and stares at his son.

"Who is she?" asks Marcello, feeling a sudden tightening in the front of his jeans. The woman is so gorgeous, she could be Miss Universe.

"Her name is Ida," says Senior. "Venetian. Junior, Ida is your new mother."

For a moment, Marcello wonders if his father is still drunk from the night before. "*You're* going to marry *her*?"

"We're married already! By proxy. I find her through a marriage broker in the Old Country. Zio Carlo, there in the picture, he stand up for me at the church. And now I got all the paperwork to bring my wife here."

"Your wife?" The facts of the situation refuse to sink into Marcello's head.

"My wife, and your mamma. How about that?"

"She looks awfully young," says Marcello, staring at Ida's face.

"Thirty-four. That's only ten years younger than me, give or take!" answers Senior, defensively.

*Thirty-four – Claudia's age.* Ida looks younger than that, but when it comes to women, Marcello knows you can't trust your eyes. Females are talented shape-changers. Christie Hryhorchuck and the other neighbourhood girls know how to add years with a little lipstick, powder and mascara. He's even seen drab canning factory girls all dolled up like movie stars to go out with their slaughterhouse-worker boyfriends. Ida can't be as pretty or as young as she appears or she wouldn't be marrying Senior. It stands to reason.

"When you're a man, what does age matter?" says Senior, pounding Marcello on the back. "It's good to be a man. Wait 'til your new mother gets here!"

Marcello holds up his hands, fending Senior off. "Hang on, Pop. She's not my mother. I'm too old for mothering."

Senior's smile disappears. He looks down at the photograph, tapping his finger again on Ida's face. "You right. She show up in a couple weeks. Maybe you leave when she comes. Not right for you to be on the pullout couch while we in the bedroom, know what I mean?"

Marcello stops what he's doing and stares at his father in disbelief. "What you expect me to do, sleep in the back alley?"

Senior shrugs. "It'll be good for you. When you go to the missions with the priests, you ain't gonna be sleeping in no comfortable bed." And with that, Senior shuffles back into the storeroom, carrying the photo of his proxy bride and a fresh issue of *Oggi*, leaving his son to sweep sprinklings of sweetness from the rough wooden floor.

# 2

*June 29*

THE VELVET CURTAINS OF the confessional are heavy with dust and shame. Marcello adjusts the chain on his scapular medal; maybe the crucifix is keeping his chest from scabbing over. Whatever the reason, the scratches from Claudia's nails are still oozing blood.

On the other side of the grillwork screen, the priest coughs lightly, peppermint mouthwash sweetening the stale air of the wooden confessional box. Marcello rouses himself to enumerate his failings.

"Bless me, Father, for I have sinned. It has been one month since my last confession and these are my sins: gambling, three-four times. Maybe five. And I beat a man, once. I didn't want to, but there was no choice."

"There's always a choice." The priest's voice is low, so no one on the other side of the box can hear. "I heard you broke Jimmy's nose."

"Just bloodied it. I might have cracked his ribs. He was trying to sneak out with our merchandise while I was restocking the storeroom."

"By 'merchandise', you mean those disgusting magazines. Why didn't you call the police?"

"Are you kidding? *Scusi*, Father, I don't mean to be disrespectful, but if I call the police, Pop and me go to jail."

Marcello can see the hands of a luminous watch dial through the grillwork screen: it's ten past three. The priest must be sitting with his head resting on his fist, one ear toward Marcello, the other toward God. The priest shifts and sighs in the darkness. "Anything else?" His voice sounds a little weary.

Marcello's mouth tastes like dust. "Adultery. Once." He searches his conscience, trying to find genuine remorse. Making a bad confession would be piling sin on sin. His one regret is his failure to stop Kowalchuck from pressuring Claudia to make good on her debt, the sex with Marcello being – in Kowalchuck's view – her own damn fault. It's as close as Marcello can get to penitence and he hopes God understands.

"I'll never do adultery again. For these and all the sins of my past life, I am heartily sorry."

To his relief, Father Ray mumbles an absolution, his luminous watch dial moonlike in the darkness as he moves his hand in blessing. But before Marcello can rise from the kneeler, the priest says: "I want to talk to you later."

Marcello pushes aside the curtain and steps into the stillness of St. Dismas Church, the only place where he sees evidence of the hand of God. Unlike the chaotic neighbourhood it serves, the interior of the church has a rational beauty that Marcello finds comforting. The apse is symmetrical, all stained glass and wood, the dome above the altar as elegant as the solution to a physics problem, the air – free of slaughterhouse smells – scented with lemon wax and a trace of incense from morning mass. In the choir loft, an organist is practicing Bach's *Air on a G String*.

He slides into a pew to pray – to God the Father, his favourite member of the Holy Trinity. The music helps his mind fly up to the loft and into the dome, away from his bloody chest and the tourniquet of guilt tightening inside his head. Aside from science books and craps games, the church is the only place where he can escape the void, that empty, windy nothingness that has slouched beside him since childhood.

He usually feels washed clean after leaving the box, a feeling that stays with him on the walk home past the ugly stucco cottages and broken-down stoops and bunker-like storefronts, full of shell-shocked DPs who all come from somewhere else and don't want to live in the purgatory of Canal Road any longer than they have to. But today, even after making confession, he feels less than pure. When did sin and forgiveness become so complicated?

He kneels to say his penance: two Our Fathers, two Hail Marys. Kid stuff. He knows the real penance will come out of the box with Father Ray, who obviously isn't buying his act of contrition for beating up Jimmy. True, there was a certain satisfaction in it: the guy staggered into the store drunk and told Marcello he'd shot a Wop who looked just like him in the War. When there's trouble with guys like Jimmy, it's usually about the War; in this neighbourhood, there's always someone who used to be enemies with someone else. Twenty-five years ago they were training their gun sights on one another, now they're supposed to be neighbourly. Jimmy particularly hates Italians, he says, first because they're Catholics and second because they're cowards – everybody knows that, he told Marcello, brandishing the stolen magazine in his fist. So yes, Marcello did need to nip the pilfering in the bud. But perhaps punching Jimmy in the face and then throwing him off the stoop held too much satisfaction in it. At least he didn't hit him with the bat. Marcello is still thinking this over when Father Ray slides in beside him.

"Two chairs, no waiting," says the priest, with a small smile.

"Hey, Father," says Marcello, tensing up at Father Ray's attempt to relax him with a joke. The priest is afraid of him now? He's a Polish guy, a former star in Junior A hockey, young enough to be Marcello's older brother. He grew up on the street.

Father Ray rests his elbows on his knees and speaks in an undertone. "I'm not sure you're serious about your calling."

Marcello closes his eyes: so he hasn't been forgiven, after all. His chest is on fire but he's almost enjoying the pain: it's a distraction from the knowledge that he's stuck in time, like Superman flying against the rotation of the earth. "Father, I'm dead serious about the seminary. I'd like to go even sooner than the fall. Pop is remarrying. I mean, he *has* remarried, a proxy bride from Italy. There isn't room for all of us in the flat."

Father Ray puts his hand on Marcello's shoulder. "I'll see what I can do to speed things up. In the mean time, strive to live a more saintly life."

Marcello returns to an empty store – empty of Pop, that is, who is making a smuggling run over the border for Kowalchuck.

At the magazine rack, Christie Hryhorchuck and the Donato twins are thumbing through *Mademoiselle* and *Miss Chatelaine* with Scripto-stained fingers. Senior has said to never let the girls touch them without paying first – *This ain't a library* – but Marcello ignores his father's orders. It's not like the girls are abusing anything serious like *Popular Science*. Besides, they keep Marcello company while he's filling time rebuilding his mother's old phonograph or playing chess, usually against himself. Marcello White versus Marcello Black.

Taking his place behind the counter, he tries not to stare at Judy and Jane Donato, miniature versions of Claudia. The girls are dressed for a majorette competition in white tasseled boots, fringed halter-tops and spangled shorts. He's sure their mother wouldn't have breathed a word to them. For his part, Marcello talked to Kowalchuck, explaining that, as far as Claudia was concerned, her debt – her husband Al's debt, it turns out – had been settled. *Basta.* Enough.

Kowalchuck laughed and said that Marcello should thank him for letting him have one on the house. When Marcello insisted that Claudia's feelings be respected, Kowalchuck's voice grew cold. He told Marcello to mind his own business. He might even decide to drop in on Claudia himself, he said. Al Donato had a weakness for slow horses and owed him big-time. Hanging up the phone, Marcello noticed blood soaking through his shirt: he taped the scratches on his chest and tried to forget his promise to Claudia.

Marcello scoops caramels and jujubes onto the weigh scale as the twins sidle up to the counter. "Hey Cello, are you going to call your Pop's new wife 'Mamma'? asks Jane.

He tries to keep his voice steady. "Ida is not my mother. She's my stepmother, I guess."

"Is she a wicked stepmother?" Jane wants to know.

Judy picks up on her twin sister's thought. "Yeah, Cello! Like in a fairytale."

Christie puts her hand on Judy's arm. "Stop bugging Cello. It's not his fault his father is old-fashioned."

"It's got nothing to do with being old-fashioned," says Marcello, coming to Pop's defense. "He's lonely, that's all."

"Yeah, but proxy marriages are so…" Judy waves her hands in the air, trying to find the word – "…backward? Proxy brides were okay back in the olden days ten years ago when Canadian girls wouldn't go near Italian men, but come on, it's almost Nineteen Seventy! You shouldn't be able to buy a woman like something out of the Eaton's Catalogue anymore. That's what my Mom says, anyway."

"Oh, yeah?" says Marcello. He tries not to show that his feelings are hurt that Claudia has been discussing his and his father's business. "Can I get you guys anything else? I've got work to do."

Sighing theatrically, the twins stuff the magazines haphazardly back in the display rack and saunter out. Christie lingers, playing with the screen door; the bell gently tinkles as she rocks it back and forth. "There's a *Gunsmoke* two-parter tonight. My folks'll be watching TV for two straight hours. Want to hang out?" At Marcello's smile of agreement, Christie lets the door bang shut in an explosion of dust motes.

At exactly five minutes to eight, he hangs the SORRY, WE'RE CLOSED sign on the door. Everyone's windows are open, an early heat wave mixing with the grit and smog of the nearby chemical plants to make the air soupy and sluggish. Tonight everyone will just want to lie on their sofas and sweat.

Marcello slips down the narrow space that separates the candy store from Christie's house, a high wooden fence between them. The boards are rotting but they block the view of the back alley. He doesn't want the Hryhorchucks to know what he and Christie are up to; Mr. H. is an outwardly jovial man who runs a religious icon shop but Marcello has heard shouts and pleading in the night, bruises visible under Christie's Cover Girl in the morning.

He finds her waiting for him, smoking a Du Maurier by the fence. "Want one?"

"Later. Let's get in the car."

Christie and Marcello have known one another since they were little; he thought of her as a kid sister until, like a hothouse orchid raised in manure, she bloomed overnight.

This past winter, the two of them developed a routine, meeting in the Chevy's back seat to feel up one another in the freezing darkness through thick wool and heavy denim. As spring warmed the air, they'd started taking their shirts off to fondle one another, but not tonight: Marcello doesn't want her to see the scratches on his chest. Instead he lies fully clothed but fully erect on top of Christie. Floating from someone's TV on the warm night air, Miss Kitty's throaty voice says *Hold your horses, cowboy.*

Christie pushes his hands away. "You know what my father would do if you got me pregnant?"

Marcello tucks her long black hair behind one ear. So thick, so soft. "The hell with your father, I'd marry you," he says, surprised to find he means it.

Christie narrows her eyes, almond-shaped and kohl rimmed. "But who says I want to marry *you*? I want to get out of here, maybe go to university."

Marcello snorts. "You say that now but you'll want to get married and have babies one day."

Christie reaches into her shirt pocket for her cigarettes. "Who made you God? Haven't you heard of women's lib?"

*Great: now Christie is getting complicated.* Marcello pulls himself up on the seat and leans back his head. Straightening her clothing, Christie joins him. "Why are you so sad?"

"I'm not sad, I'm frustrated. Can I have one of your smokes?"

The two sit side-by-side, not touching. The tips of their cigarettes flare in the darkness. Marcello can hear the sound of a commercial floating in the humid air: *Cheer gets whites whiter and colours brighter!*

"Ever notice how none of the places on TV are like Canal Road?" asks Christie. "I'd love to live in that town on *My Three Sons.*"

"I'll be leaving soon, because of my Pop's proxy bride coming," says Marcello.

"You're lucky," says Christie.

Marcello touches the fresh bruise on Christie's cheek, a memento of Mr. Hryhorchuck's latest drunken tantrum.

"I can make him stop," states Marcello.

Christie snorts. "What you going to do, Cello, scare him? Or beat him up?"

Marcello's face must have registered shame because she takes his hand: "It's sweet of you, but I just want to get out of here. Don't complicate things."

Christie goes home just before ten and Marcello heads back to the store's front stoop. *Channel 7 Eyewitness News* is on next door, another three-alarm fire burning in downtown Buffalo. Canal Road is empty but male voices float on the night air.

He crosses the street and slips through a narrow space between Kowalchuck's Flower Shop and Vito's Shoe Repair, emerging into a pool of yellow light thrown by a kerosene lantern. A dozen guys are ganged at the back of the flower shop, tossing dice against a chalk circle drawn on a brick wall, a cash-stuffed ball cap on the ground in front of them. When Marcello walks out of the shadows, the players stand up as one man, ready to run; when they see it's him, they all sit down again.

As usual, Stinky is supervising the game, his left arm blue with tattoos, the right arm ending in a ragged stump just below the elbow. His nickname comes from working at the foul-smelling meat packers for fifteen years, where he lost his forearm in a cutting machine.

"Have a seat, kid. Got something for you." Stinky pulls a thick roll of bills from his pants pocket, secured by an elastic band. Holding the wad of money between his knees, he peels off two twenties and a ten. "A gift from the Bank of Kowalchuck."

"Gift?" Marcello knows this is bullshit. "If I lose, I don't know if I'll be able to pay it back."

"So don't lose."

To his relief, Marcello wins his first roll, and the next, then loses, then wins, then settles into a losing streak that burns through all the borrowed cash within fifteen minutes.

The players around him crouch like animals tracking prey, arms bulging and knuckles popping as they shake and roll the dice. Even with no money to stake, the rhythm of the men's voices, the bottle of rye being passed from hand to mouth, and the clicking of the dice keep Marcello company. Most are old guys in their thirties or forties, except for Marcello and a skinny kid, bright with acne, of eleven or twelve who hangs around on the outer rim of the players' circle, following the action. 'Bum Bum'. His mother goes door to door on Canal Road, dragging the kid with her in his mud coloured clothing and orange little-girl sneakers, trying to bum cash from neighbours, including Senior. "*Signore, my boy is hungry, my husband loses all his money at craps.*" But of course Senior always sends her on her way with a wave of his hand. Thanks to his mother, Bum Bum (real name: Pasquale) has a talent for begging, something the craps players exploit by sending him out to bum cigarettes, money and booze from friends up and down the street, bringing his loot back to the chalk circle for a chance to play or a share of the booze. Bumming for the craps players is how the kid got his nickname, or so Marcello hopes: there's been some snickering among the neighbourhood teenagers that the name means something else, something to do with Bum Bum's Pop getting him drunk on homemade wine and lending him out to a couple of guys he owed money to. Marcello tries not to even look at the kid.

Tonight an old guy is in on the game, Stan, a biker from Hamilton, revered as a runner-up in the *Mister Man of Steel Contest*, back in 1955. Stinky claims that *even though Stan don't body-build no more, punching him in the gut is like slamming your fist into a brick wall*, but when Stan crouches to roll the dice, fish-belly fat overflows the back of his leathers and he wheezes when he calls his numbers. His tobacco-stained beard stands out in white bristles, like Pappy in the comic strip *L'il Abner*. Stan keeps Bum Bum busy, running back and forth on scabbed, skinny legs, borrowing a buck here, five bucks there from the other players, Stan rewarding the kid with shots of rye and the odd hair ruffle.

After too many losing rolls and turns at the bottle, Marcello sways to his feet and heads to the concrete pad of a back-alley garage; long abandoned, it's the accepted place for defecation and quick ones with girls from the pool hall. Bladder aching, Marcello staggers toward the garage. When he comes around the corner, he sees Stan, leather pants around his knees, hand busy on his crotch.

Marcello is about to tell him to jerk off somewhere else, when he sees that the biker's hand is gripping something soft and round, a small head bobbing up and down, up and down, in front of him. Bum Bum kneels before the man's trembling thighs, his hands splayed like a monkey's as he braces his arms wide against the fence, his orange sneakered feet tucked in at the toes like a little kid at prayer. He's too short to kneel and too tall to stand, so he works away at Stan in this painful-looking, half-crucified crouch. Marcello wonders if the stance offers some special pleasure to the boy or the biker or both, until he realizes it's just physics, Bum Bum counterbalancing so he doesn't topple into the trash.

Stan's eyes open, catching Marcello's look. "Wait your turn, Junior," he grunts.

Marcello steps back into the shadows and staggers up the alley and out into the streetlights of Canal Road. Giving up the idea of privacy – *what's that, a civilized concept, come on* – he exposes himself in the open, releasing a pent-up stream of urine into the gutter near a hydrant. Watching the rivulets trickle away into the storm sewer, he feels both self-revulsion and relief.

*What difference does it make, there's no one on the street anyway.*

*That's not the point,* some other part of him insists, *if everyone does it, Canal Road will turn into a toilet.*

*Yeah well that seems to be happening anyway, so what difference does it make if I hurry the process along?*

Gradually, the men drift away as daylight fills the alley; a few curl up to sleep against the wall, passed out from too much rye, Bum Bum among them, his face looking chapped and raw. The biker has vanished. A couple of men sneak into the flower shop to steal a cup of old lady Kowalchuck's Maxwell House before they head to the foundry.

Stinky hands Marcello the bottle of Canadian Club, a few fingers of rye still sloshing around on the bottom. "Kowalchuck was impressed with the way you worked Jimmy over. He wants to talk to you about another job."

Marcello touches his chest; the pain is back. *A warning*, he thinks.

"What I did to Jimmy wasn't a job, it was just something I had to do."

Stinky shrugs and smiles. "Same thing. Go get some sleep."

Marcello drains the CC and winds his way back to the candy store, a little springy in the legs like a Slinky on a broken stairway.

The next afternoon, with Marcello at the counter nursing a hangover with aspirin and prayer, Bum Bum sticks his head into the store, causing the door chime to ring. Standing half-in, half-out of the doorway, he brings with him a stink of unwashed flesh. The boy's black eyes roll over Marcello like wet marbles.

"I seen you with that girl."

Marcello's breath quickens. "What girl?" He wants to be sure Bum Bum isn't bullshitting him.

The kid nods in the direction of the Hryhorchucks' house. "Old Ukrainian guy's girl. Skinny chick."

Shit. Bum Bum must have peeked into the back of the Chevy on his way to the craps game. If Mr. H. hears about this and punishes Christie, Marcello will be at fault. Sticking his hand into a box of wrapped caramels, he scoops out a handful into a small bag, then twists it closed and extends it toward Bum Bum. The kid takes it but stares at Marcello like a hungry dog.

"Licorice."

Marcello throws a licorice pipe into a second bag, adds another, then tosses in a handful of Lik'M Ades for good measure. He's giving away a half-day's wages but he wants the kid gone. More importantly, he wants him to keep his mouth shut. Bum Bum takes the second bag with an astonished grin. This is more than he expected. He starts for the door, then hesitates, deciding to hand Marcello a piece of information by way of making change.

"That Italian chick your Pop marry – *come si chiama?*"

"Ida."

"*Si, Ida.* Kowalchuck pay her way."

Now it's Marcello's turn to hesitate. "You sure?"

Bum Bum nods. "Heard him say Senior owes him big-time."

Marcello suspects Bum Bum is bullshitting him. He hardens his voice: "Go away, Pasquale. Stop spying on me or I'll beat you up."

His mouth drooling caramel juice, Bum Bum is already out the door. Marcello stands in the dusty silence, gripping the counter in confusion. Then he grabs the door and slams it open, the spring groaning. "Pasquale!"

The boy turns and stares at Marcello, skinny legs poised to run again. Marcello looks up and down the street. No one's around. "I'll break your arms if you say anything to anyone about what you saw in my car. Now get the hell out of here."

Bum Bum grins and saunters away.

# 3

*July 1*

MARCELLO AWAKES TO AN orange sky streaked with acid yellow clouds. *Must be off-gassing at DuPont,* he thinks. Trapped between the chemical plants of upstate New York and Canadian steel plants to the east, Shipman's Corners can be as smoggy as a city. The surrounding farms and factories add their emissions of DDTs and PCBs to the toxic alphabet soup. Rumours are even starting to circulate about a neighbourhood on the other side of the river where babies are being born with giant heads like something out of a horror movie. With all his scientific reading, Marcello quietly suspects that the town is poisoning itself: another good reason to leave.

After an early morning mass, he helps his father shave and dress, even ironing a shirt for him. Senior's got the shakes. He was up late again last night with the Hiram Walker – liquid courage, Marcello suspects. *How long has it been since Pop was with a woman?* As he knots a soup-stained tie around his father's neck, he tries to stop imagining the old man making love to Claudia.

"I look okay?" asks Senior, lifting his chin in front of the crazed mirror in the flat's single bedroom.

"You look good," Marcello reassures him, patting his back. What is he supposed to say?

After Senior leaves for the airport in Kowalchuck's Impala, Marcello starts getting the place ready for Ida's welcome party. As he moves boxes into the storeroom, he wonders if the sky is trying to tell him something. What's that old saying, something about a warning and a red sky in the morning?

The Andolinis arrive early in a parade of cars led by a Caddy carrying Prima and her oldest son, followed by a string of late-model Regals, Corvairs and Ramblers; the family must be doing well. No sooner have their cars lined the curb than

Prima and the other Andolini women jump out and start unloading cleaning supplies; they clatter up the fire escape to the two-room flat above the store, strip Senior's sagging bed and carry the sheets to the coin laundry – Marcello can't remember the last time they were washed. The women scrub the cracked linoleum floor and wipe down the ancient fridge, inside and out, with diluted bleach, Marcello nervously hovering and warning them to take care; with its exposed condenser coils, the fridge isn't even grounded, making it a shock hazard. The women laugh and wave him off with soapy yellow-gloved hands; *you're a good boy but you always worry too much, carino – stop trying to help us and go sit with the men!* They've cooked lasagna and spaghetti with spicy sausages at home and brought everything with them to rewarm in the oven – a good thing, because only one burner on the rusty old Moffat stove still works. Meanwhile, the Andolini men set up folding tables and chairs on the sidewalk where they lounge drinking Red Caps while the women run back and forth at their work. Someone gets out a deck of cards.

Marcello runs an extension cord down the front steps of the store and sets up his record player in the open air; it's a bit of a Frankenstein, cobbled together from the turntable of his mother's old phonograph and bits and pieces of cast-off hi-fis that he's picked up for almost nothing at the junk shop. Not too pretty but it does the job. Marcello starts things off with selections from *Carmen* but the Andolinis pronounce opera too serious for the occasion and start spinning their own LPs: Dean Martin, Louis Prima, Connie Francis, Frank Sinatra, Vic Damone.

"Now *that's* music," approves Prima, nodding her battleship-grey head in time to Sinatra crooning "Fly Me to the Moon" as she climbs the fire escape with a basket of towels.

Niagara Glen Kowalchuck leans against the railing of the candy store stoop, arms crossed, watching the women work and the men drink beer and ante up. He's dressed in blue jeans, cowboy boots and an embroidered rodeo shirt, his buttercup-blonde hair slicked back from his forehead and worn long over the collar, a bandanna tight around his neck like Elvis in *Viva Las Vegas*. He's even got the sneer down pat. With the empty blue eyes of a husky dog, he gazes confidently out at the street, a king surveying his realm. When Gina Andolini, one of Prima's younger, prettier daughters-in-law, hurries up the stoop with a basket of laundry, Kowalchuck reaches out to her with a "Hello darlin'" – Marcello thinks, at first, to help her with the basket – but instead he slaps her buttocks as she passes. "*Ma che!*" Gina says and, heaving the weight of the basket onto one hip, swats him away good-naturedly. Kowalchuck chuckles. Noticing Marcello, he gives a quick nod and says: "Big day."

Marcello crosses his arms, mirroring Kowalchuck's body language. "I hear you gave Pop the money to bring Ida over."

"Where'd you hear that?"

"Pasquale told me." When Kowalchuck looks puzzled, Marcello adds: "Bum Bum."

"That kid should learn to keep his mouth shut."

"Why'd you pay her way?"

Kowalchuck shrugs. "Your Pop lost his get-up-and-go when your mother died a couple years back."

"It's been fourteen years since my mother died," Marcello reminds him.

"No shit? Time flies. Anyways, he wanted to get back on the horse. I floated him a loan so he could marry a girl from home. Someone who does what she's told. Not like the ball-busters here."

Marcello shifts uncertainly from foot to foot; he wants to understand exactly what his father's gotten himself into. "Pop owes you, then."

Kowalchuck looks back to the street where one of the Andolini men has rolled his cards to the groans of his fellow players. "Everybody owes me. Which reminds me, Stinky says your account's over two hunnert as of last night. I got a job for you. Be a good way to pay off your debts."

Marcello should have seen this coming. Remembering Father Ray's advice to live a more saintly life, he says, "I'm not going to start scaring people for money."

"Come on, you'll enjoy it. He's a rich shit out in the country who won't pay his bills. But this ain't the time to talk. It's a party, right?" he says, slapping Marcello's back.

The party draws neighbours from all along Canal Road. The Hryhorchucks arrive with a bowl of perogies and a bottle of homemade onion Vodka, Christie carrying a poppyseed cake she made herself. Even the Donatos show up: Claudia, her sport-jacketed husband Al, and Jane and Judy in their white boots and spangled shorts. Eyes lowered, Claudia hands Marcello a Jell-O salad with carrots and peas floating like sea monkeys in a thick lime ocean.

It's the first time he's seen her since that day with the TV; looking at her now in her demure mini-dress and pumps, a white bow in her bouffant hairdo, he can't help thinking of her rocking back and forth on his lap, riding him like a horse. Her nails are even painted that same creamsicle orange. An itchy warmth starts to spread over his chest: *not here, not now*, he prays, crossing his arms.

"How are you?" he asks.

"Lousy. You didn't keep your promise," she says in her soft, raspy voice.

Marcello is starting to think Kowalchuck was right. Claudia made the mistake, not him. Stepping back he says: "Nothing more I can do. I'll be leaving soon, to go into the priesthood."

Claudia waves a hand at him dismissively. "Priest, my ass. You're as bad as the rest of them. If he touches the twins, it'll be on your head, Lollipop."

She turns her back on Marcello to join her daughters. Feeling a warm trickle of blood under his shirt, he heads inside to apply a trail of Band-Aids to the scratches on his chest.

The Impala pulls up in front of the candy store at exactly three in the afternoon with a small figure in the back seat, head erect. Senior, stuffed into his too-tight suit and out-of-date fedora, hauls himself out of the driver side door, face twitching with the effort to smile. He looks like someone out of the funny papers, a cartoon of a chauffeur holding open the back door of the car. He does everything short of salute.

When Ida steps out of the Impala, Marcello hears a blast of Vivaldi's "Summer" from *The Four Seasons* swirling inside his head and his eyes are dazzled by tiny sparks of light. He thinks that they might be from the heat wave, or glare off the chrome of the car, or perhaps an optical illusion caused by the refraction of sunlight through heavy particulates in smoggy air blown in from the American side of the border. Whatever the reason, Ida emerges onto the dusty sidewalk of Canal Road in a shower of what appears to be fairy dust. Marcello's first thought is: *What the hell is she doing here?* To him, she looks like an angel – or maybe a goddess – who muddled her directions and went badly off course during her descent to Earth.

To the others gathered in front of the candy store, Ida looks like a short, pale woman with blonde hair scraped off her face into a tight little bun. Pretty enough, but no beauty queen. She wears her prim clothes – a beige knee-length skirt, white blouse, and square-toed *peau de soie* pumps – with the self-conscious posture of a department store mannequin. She looks like a woman carved out of ice. Everyone freezes in place like pieces on a chessboard rather than rushing forward to greet her warmly.

Prima claps her hands to break the spell. "*Brava, brava!*" she says, untying her apron and pulling Ida into her arms. Ida laughs and pats the old woman's shoulders, but doesn't hug her back.

Senior gently pulls Ida away from Prima and begins to lead her around, making introductions. The women kiss her carefully on her powdered cheeks. The men shake her hands by the fingertips, afraid to crush her.

Marcello, still dizzied by the Venetian baroque music swirling in his head, comes back to life when he hears Gina muttering to Prima, "What is a girl like that doing with Senior?"

Prima replies: "*Non lo so.* I don't know. Maybe it's business."

"Ah," says Gina, as if this explains everything.

Marcello watches as Senior introduces Ida to Niagara Glen Kowalchuck. The creep takes her hand and kisses it like some type of fricken Count from a horror movie. That's who he reminds Marcello of: not Elvis. Dracula.

"Pleasure," Kowalchuck says, his husky eyes walking all over Ida, not just her face, but her body too. Ida's smile disappears and she takes a step back.

*She's afraid of him*, thinks Marcello.

"*Piacere*," she whispers finally, then turns to be introduced to the next person.

Finally, Senior escorts Ida to Marcello, her hand tucked into the old man's elbow.

"…And this is Marcello *Junior*," says Senior, patting his son on the back. "Your stepson. As you see, he's too big for mothering!"

Ida's eyes widen in obvious surprise – "*Mah no,* this is the child you wrote of?" – but she recovers quickly and gives a little laugh, covering her mouth in a strangely old-ladyish gesture, like a *nonna* hiding her dentures. "I expect a wee boy but you, Marcello, you are not little! But no one is too old to be cared for, yes?" She speaks a precise, softly accented, Britishy English, as if she learned to speak from the Queen. When she gets up on tiptoe and brushes his cheek with her lips, Marcello wonders if she can hear his heart beat.

"I am so very happy to meet you," she says, her hands on her stepson's chest.

Sweatered and slippered, Maria Cocco and Angela So-and-So, neighbourhood ladies of about Senior's age, corner Ida. Angela seizes her hand: "Maria and I marry our husbands by proxy too."

"I cried the first time I saw Canada," Maria chimes in. "And when I seen my new husband I cried even harder."

Angela keeps a bony grip on Ida's wrist, drawing her close. "Tell your husband to let you settle in first," she says, her voice intense. "He should not touch you for at least a month!"

Maria nods. "Get used to things first. There's plenty of time for the rest of it."

"*Grazie, signora,*" says Ida, glancing at Marcello, her discomfort obvious. She's trying to move on but Angela won't let go of her hand.

"We here if you need us," says Angela, finally letting go. "It's hard, it's very hard to marry a man you no ever meet and come to a country where you no have family. We be your family now."

Introductions made, Senior and the other men return to their beer and cards. Ida takes a seat with the women in a semicircle of kitchen chairs on the sidewalk in front of the store. She's so cool and correct, so proper, crossing her legs demurely at the ankles, her hands overlapping carefully in her lap, that none of the women quite know what to make of her.

Christie asks where she learned to speak such good English and Ida shrugs and says, "I have what you call the ear for language."

Marcello can hear the whispers of the Andolini women – in their dialect, so there's no chance the Venetian goddess will understand:

"*She doesn't even look Italian! Swiss, maybe.*"

"*They look like that, that bunch up north. Like Heidi.*"

"*Have you ever heard an accent as strange as hers?*"

"*And the way she speaks English – she sounds like a snob!*"

"*She holds herself a little too high.*"

"*Her husband will put her in her place, soon enough.*"

When Ida complains of thirst, Marcello jumps up and goes into the store for a Coke, Christie following him inside. "How old is your stepmother supposed to be?"

Marcello winces at the word 'stepmother'. "Thirty-four."

Christie whisks the bottle out of his hand and snaps off the cap on the cooler's opener. "Wake up, Cello! Senior robbed the cradle."

When Marcello goes back outside and offers the overflowing Coke to Ida, she accepts it with a smile worthy of a toothpaste commercial: "*Grazie,* Marcello! But your father is Marcello also. How does one know both of you apart?"

"We call him 'Cello' because he likes classical music," volunteers Christie.

"Cello? A splendid name for you, I think!" says Ida, but her words are interrupted by the blast of a siren: "*Cosa succede? What goes on?*"

Marcello points toward the superstructure of a saltie gliding quietly above the fields backing onto Canal Road. "*Guarda.* It's the siren for the bridge going up so a ship can pass. They sail through here from all over the world."

"*Andiamo!* Let's go!"

Surprised by her eagerness to leave the party, Marcello tells Senior that he's taking Ida for a walk. He expects his father to object, but Senior, intent on his poker hand, waves them off: "Yeah, sure, go ahead!" Kowalchuck is the only man who looks up from the game, his eyes flicking over Marcello, then back to his cards. Dismissing him.

Marcello can feel the women's eyes on Ida and him as they walk along Canal Road. The moment they are out of sight of the store, Ida stops and stifles a huge yawn. "*Allora!*" she says to the sky. "Is good to be away from all those people!"

Marcello is surprised by her rudeness: does she not realize how much trouble they went to for her? He guesses that you've got to make allowances for someone who just crossed the ocean.

"You must be beat," he suggests.

Ida frowns, not understanding. "Beat?"

"Tired. Jet-lagged. *Stanchi.*"

Ida nods and gives another huge yawn, this time not bothering to cover it. "*Si,* but is very good to stretch my legs."

At the top of the embankment, the two find themselves facing the rusty steel wall of the *Koningin Juliana*, a saltie out of Amsterdam, loaded to the plimsoll markings and leaking ballast like a bloated steel whale. The ocean-going tub is having a hard time lining up with the lift lock. Whistles, catcalls, chewing gum and cigarette packages rain down on them from above – on Ida, really.

"Sorry, Ida," says Marcello, picking up the cigarettes. "They've probably been at sea for awhile."

"Is okay, I'm used to. Men the same from everywhere," she sighs, unwrapping a stick of gum and popping it into her mouth.

Marcello helps her across a patch of gravel to a bollard for tying up ships, where she seats herself to watch the *Koningen Juliana* slide by. The ship is so close they could almost touch her. Ida pats the flat iron surface of the bollard: "Sit with me, Cello."

He likes the way she pronounces his name with a little trill: *Chay-llow.*

There's plenty of room, but they rest against one another, hips touching. He is convinced his heartbeat is echoing straight through his body into hers. He lights up one of the cigarettes: it's the usual Russian crap the foreign sailors like to throw down to the locals, but at least they're free. He offers Ida one but she shakes her head.

"Why the sailors throw us gifts?"

"The guys on salties always do that when they sail through the canal. Cigarettes, gum, candy, sometimes little toys. I figure it's some kind of offering to protect them when they're back on the open sea. Like lighting a candle in church."

"Ah, magic!" says Ida. "How you say – superstition."

"More like faith," Marcello corrects her.

With the sunshine streaming down, Marcello gazes at Ida's upturned face and considers what Christie said about her age. It's true that she appears almost childlike. Especially with a mouth full of chewing gum.

"Your father seems very nice," says Ida slowly and not very convincingly. "How old, he is?"

"Forty-five," says Marcello, suspecting that Pop lied to her about his age.

"And you – you are quite the surprise!" she volunteers. "I come here expecting a little one. A child to care for. Is there some other son?"

Marcello shakes his head, mentally noting another one of Senior's lies: a child to nurture. No wonder Ida came to Shipman's Corners. She had no idea what she was getting into.

"*Cose fai, Cello?* What do you do in your life?" asks Ida, waving to the sailors who continue to shout to her from above.

"I help my father run the store. But I'm going to be a priest."

Ida's eyebrows shoot skyward. "*Pfff! Davvero?* You want this?"

"It's not a question of *wanting.* Ever since I was little, I knew it was my calling. And the Order will send me to university."

"Ah. A practical decision. To get an education."

"It's a spiritual decision, too. I want to serve God and help the less fortunate." Marcello's words sound hollow even to himself, but he would rather not give his real reasons: guilt, obligation, and a desire for escape. Too much to tell a woman he hardly knows.

"You try to convince me or yourself?" Ida shoots back.

Marcello is surprised by the strength of her reaction: she hardly knows him but already demands that he account for himself. Old Prima had a word for girls like this: *sfacciata.* Nervy. Not a desirable quality in a woman.

"You're not religious?"

Ida shakes her head emphatically. "Growing up, I know many priests. Many of them were not religious either."

Thinking it's time to change the subject, he gets up off the bollard. "Let's watch the water pumping out of the lock. That's how the ships get around Niagara Falls."

"I have seen canals before, coming from *Venezia,*" she murmurs, absently. "But I am wondering – where are the horses?

"Horses?"

She waves her tiny hands impatiently in the air. "This is why I tell the marriage broker to seek me out a husband on the frontier. Like in the cinema. '*Il Buono, Il Brutto, Il Cattivo*'. *L'hai mai visto?*"

"Sure, I've seen *The Good, the Bad and the Ugly.* A spaghetti western."

Ida laughs and shakes her head. "Spaghetti?"

"Never mind." Marcello struggles to gently tell her the truth. "Why did you call this the 'frontier'?"

Ida sits straighter, removing her gum and sticking it to the underside of the bollard. "I read, read, read. I consult my Nonno's atlas. Shipman Corner is part of the Niagara Frontier."

Marcello would laugh at Ida's misinterpretation if it hadn't landed her in so much trouble. "That's what the Americans call it. But the word 'frontier' doesn't just mean hinterland. It can also mean being on a border. Niagara is where America turns into Canada. *Capisci?*"

Ida stares at him, her disappointment obvious in her difficulty getting out the words: "No horses?"

Marcello shakes his head. "The candy store is pretty much all my father owns."

Ida looks past Marcello at the disappearing stern of the *Koningen Juliana*. Her smile has turned into a cramped little frown, her hand twisting and untwisting the bow on her blouse. "*Ah*, I see," she says bitterly. "Too good for truth. Of course. Like always." She looks toward Lake Ontario: "Where can one go, if the boat sails that way?"

"Toronto, then Montreal, through the St. Lawrence Seaway. All the way to the Atlantic."

"'The St. Lawrence Seaway'," she says in her very precise English. "*Allora.*"

"We should probably head back," he suggests, feeling the weight of Ida's disappointment. She's only just arrived and has already been let down. Now he has to return this lovely woman – who looks more like a girl – to his lying *buffone* of a father. It's disgusting. But she's Senior's wife. There's no choice.

Back at Italian Tobacco & Sweets, the food is eaten, the wine and beer is drunk, the songs are sung, the women have washed up, the neighbours have drifted home and the Andolinis have gotten back into their flotilla of cars for the drive back to the farm. As the light dims and the party breaks up, Canada Day fireworks can be seen exploding over the lake.

While Senior fetches the luggage from the trunk of the Impala, Ida waits at the bottom of the fire escape leading to the flat. In the fast-falling darkness, Marcello can't make out the expression on her face but he can see that she's twisting her wedding ring round and round on her finger.

Senior bustles up with the bags, swaying slightly; he's drunk again. "*Avanti*, Ida! You go on up. I join you in a minute. Gotta talk to your son first."

"Good night, Cello," Ida says in a small, tight voice before clattering up the fire escape. Marcello chest aches at the sound of her going up the stairs. He grabs his father's arm, holding him in place on the stairway. "Pop, when were you planning to confess to Ida that you don't own the Ponderosa?"

Senior lifts his chin at his son. "She tell you about that, eh?"

"Why the hell did you tell her you own horses?"

Senior shrugs. "A little story to get her over here. She tell the marriage broker she want a husband with horses, so I tell her we got horses. She get used to things."

"That really stinks, Pop. Not to mention it's a mortal sin."

"What, you a priest already? She got a roof over her head, ain't she? She got no choice in the matter."

"You lied your way into marrying her. I bet a judge would say you weren't even married."

"You want to be a lawyer now on top of a priest? I got a paper from the Italian government, another one from Canada and one from the church. All of them say Ida belong to me. That mean I can do whatever I want to her. *Capisci?*"

"*Lo ti disprezzo!*" growls Marcello. "You make me ashamed to be your son."

Senior turns and heads up the stairway, scuffing Ida's white suitcases on each step. As he climbs, Marcello makes one more effort to slow him down: "Pop, Angela and Maria said you should give Ida time to settle in – a month, at least – before you expect anything of her."

Senior stops and turns toward Marcello. "*Ma che cazzo dici?* Those old biddies can go fuck themselves."

Marcello heads to the Chevy and stretches out as best he can in the back seat, jeans stuffed behind his head for a pillow. The cicadas are as loud as an orchestra, their drums and fiddles predicting another scorcher tomorrow. He tries praying but the words are overtaken by visions of Ida. Her eyes, her lips, the way she moved her hands while haranguing him about the priesthood. He reminds himself that she belongs to Senior: yes, he lied to her but he's probably not the first husband to do that.

He touches his chest. The skin is tender, but not bleeding. He finally seems to be healing up.

As he drifts off, he hears a quick, surprised intake of breath. When he opens his eyes, he can make out a small face peering into the open window. Sitting up, he smacks his head on the roof of the car.

"What the hell you doing out here?" It's Bum Bum's voice. "Your Pop throw you out? I know a better place to sleep. Nice, soft grass in front of the church. Nobody bother you under the big cross."

Marcello rubs his head. It's as though God has sent Bum Bum to remind him that yes, things could be worse. He's about to send the kid away with a threat and a curse but stops himself: it's not his fault he's an outcast. And right now he seems to be trying to help.

"It's okay, Pasquale. I'm fine here." Then adds, "Thanks."

"No problem, man. You need me bum something for you, you tell me. Us boys living outside, we gotta stick together. Gets dangerous some time."

Marcello looks at the kid: he can't be more than twelve, tops. "Your folks have a house, don't they? Why don't you sleep there instead of at the church?"

Bum Bum's grin disappears; his face hardens into a tough little acne-scarred mask. "My Pop's friends always there, bugging me, teasing me. And my Nonna, she yell too much." He looks suspicious. "Why the hell you want me go home?"

Marcello holds up his hands as if in surrender: "Most people would rather sleep in a bed than on the ground."

Bum Bum peers through the window at Marcello folded into the back seat.

"Look who talks," he says, walking backwards away from the Chevy.

Marcello can hear the sound of the boy skipping all the way down the alley.

# 4

*July 2*

MARCELLO WAKES WITH THE sun full in his face, his muscles stiff from sleeping on the Chevy's cramped back seat. He reaches up and touches the goose egg on his forehead. At least the pain on his chest has disappeared. Gently probing the skin of his chest with his fingertips, he is relieved to find nothing unusual.

Hunger and the need to urinate finally get him to his feet and drive him into the candy store. Neither he or Pop thought to lock up last night. Expecting silence, he is surprised to hear the usual television sounds coming from the storeroom.

Opening the door, he sees Senior sitting on the cot in his bathrobe with a pillow and one of the freshly laundered sheets. "What are you doing down here?"

Senior lifts his chin at him; he's got a bag of Freezies on his head. "What kind of man you think I am?" he asks gruffly. "I'm giving my wife time to settle in. You can't just jump all over a woman like that. She's not some *puttana*."

Marcello sits down next to his father. The odour of rye is strong in the room but Marcello isn't sure whether it's coming from Senior or from whatever he spilled on the floor last night. "How long?"

"Ida say, a month is traditional for a proxy marriage." Senior stretches and grins. "It's good to have a nice, traditional Italian wife. Like your *mamma*, rest in peace. Ida even feel bad that you lose your bed cause of her."

"Very considerate of her," agrees Marcello. "I'll go upstairs and see if she needs anything."

"Good, good," says Senior, his attention returning to the TV.

Marcello climbs the fire escape to the flat. Through the screen door, he sees Ida, her hair loose to her shoulders, sitting at the Formica table with one of the chipped china cups in front of her. Her face is in her hands: Marcello realizes she is crying. He considers turning around and going quietly back downstairs, then reminds himself that she's far from her family; she's probably just homesick and could use a shoulder to lean on. He knocks at the door.

When Ida looks up at him, he expects to see her face streaked with tears, but she looks like he's interrupted her deep in thought: a sheet of paper is spread on the table in front of her. It takes a moment to register that she's looking at a map. When Ida sees Marcello, she quickly folds and stuffs it into the pocket of her robe.

"*Buona mattina*," he says, wishing her good morning through the screen very formally.

"Good day!" she says brightly, not afraid to answer his Italian with her formal English. Marcello is beginning to suspect she's not afraid of much of anything.

"Okay if I come in?"

Ida gives a quick nod, smoothing her hands over her hair. "*Certo!* This your home, too."

Despite this little reassurance, Marcello walks in quietly and sits down across from her slowly, as if she's an animal he's met in the wild, ready to bolt at one wrong move.

"You found coffee," he says.

She peers into the cup. "I think so, but when I try to brew it on the stove, it tastes bad."

"That's Nescafe. Instant coffee. You just boil water in the kettle and mix it up in your cup."

Ida's face collapses into an expression of disgust. "*Beh!* This is sacrilege."

Marcello bursts out laughing. "I can help you choose some good coffee later, if you like, after ten when the stores open. Okay?"

"*D'accordo*," says Ida, checking her wristwatch. "I forget to change time."

"What time is it in Italy right now?" he asks.

She yawns as she slips the watch off her wrist. "One in afternoon. Time for lunch. My brother Rico will be getting ready to serve the guests. My Nonno will be missing me. He goes to chase away the stragglers at this hour so that I can make beds." She twists the stem of the watch again and again, going backwards six hours; Marcello suspects she would like to go even further back in time. After a night in Senior's sagging bed, in the windowless bedroom of the two-room flat, she probably wishes she had never left home.

"Your family runs a hotel?" asks Marcello.

Ida waves her hands as if trying to pull words from their air: "A *pensione*, more correctly."

"What did they think of your marriage to Pop?" he asks, curious about why such an attractive young woman, working in a *pensione* in a city like Venice, full of history and churches and art, would ever want to leave for a place like Shipman's Corners.

Ida looks down into the whiteness of her lap and presses her fingers to her eyes. The gesture reminds him uncomfortably of Claudia rubbing her contact lenses. Ida's forthrightness seems to have drained out of her overnight.

"*Non lo so*," she mumbles through her fingers. "I leave a note two days ago, before I take the train for Milano where is the plane. My *Nonno* must find it, must *have* found it, by now."

"You mean, you didn't get their permission to leave?" Marcello is deeply shocked. How could a woman disregard her family's feelings and just disappear? Perhaps something is wrong with Ida. How else to explain running away from her own blood, leaving nothing behind but a letter?

As if reading his mind, Ida puts her hand over her mouth and gives what sounds like a hiccup but is actually, Marcello realizes, a sob. "*Scusci, scusi*," she whispers, pressing the cloth belt of her robe to her eyes.

Marcello looks at her uncomfortably, uncertain what to do: go get one of the other proxy brides to talk to her? They'd probably be as confused as he is by an Italian woman with no regard for either the church or her family. She might as well as come from Mars. He supposes he could comfort her himself, maybe wrap his arms around her, let her cry against his chest?

Sensing danger in these thoughts, he stands up: "I'm going to go get Pop and then fix you something to eat. Okay? You'll feel better if you eat something."

Ida shakes her head and stands up too. She's wearing a long white cloth robe; these light colours seem to be all she wears, making her seem even paler. "No, no, I am the wife and mother and now, I will make the breakfast for the two of you. You are my family, this is only proper. If you have eggs, I make *omeletti*."

"Okay then," agrees Marcello, relieved. He doesn't really know how to cook: all he would have done was spread some Nutella on bread toasted over a stove burner. He runs down the stairs to get Pop; the heat and humidity has already started to build, the air so thick you can taste the grit in it. In the distance, Marcello can see the glow of flaring smokestacks.

By the time he gets downstairs, Senior is almost dressed; he's pulled his suspenders over a reasonably clean shirt and managed to wet and comb his hair at the storeroom sink. He looks like hell, though, his face haggard and stubbled, his eyes bloodshot.

"She up?" mumbles Senior, adjusting his suspenders. "How I look?"

Marcello turns Senior's shirt collar right side in. "She's awake, but she's feeling a little homesick. She's going to make us breakfast. Give her a few minutes to get dressed, then we'll go upstairs."

Senior smiles. "Breakfast! See? Didn't I tell you it would be good to have a woman to do for us again?"

"Yeah, Pop, you did. Now let's see if we can make you a little more presentable."

After running a comb through his father's hair and giving him a shave, Marcello digs out an ancient bottle of Old Spice from under the sink. Patting it on Senior's face, Marcello judges him as ready as he'll ever be to greet his bride.

They go to the fire escape and he gestures to his father: "You first."

In the flat, they find Ida looking crisp in a white blouse and capri pants, her hair tugged off her face with a yellow hairband. Having dried her eyes and dabbed on a bit of lipstick, she's tying on a ruffled apron the Andolini women left behind for her. *Good*, thinks Marcello. *She's getting used to things.*

"Good morning! *Mangiare*," says Ida; she's set three places at the table using chipped china plates and threadbare cloth napkins that date from Sofia's time. Hoisting a battered frypan, she slides an omelet onto each plate. There's coffee, too: Ida has grudgingly boiled water and made the instant coffee according to Marcello's instructions.

Marcello doesn't think he's ever sat at the old Formica table properly set before; it's all amazingly civilized. He cuts a perfectly browned corner of the omelet and tastes it while Ida stands beside him, waiting for his reaction.

"Oh man. This is probably the best thing anyone's made in here since, since…" *Since my mother died*, he thinks, but leaves the thought unfinished. "*Grazie*, Ida."

"*Prego*. If you want to thank me, perhaps take me some place to buy the good coffee."

"I'll ask Maria Cocco where to go. Pop and I pretty much make do with what we sell in the store."

After cleaning up from breakfast, Marcello takes a few bucks from the till and tells his father that he's taking Ida shopping. "For some kitchen things. Things she needs to, you know, be a good wife."

"Good, good," says Senior, waving them off.

Their first stop is at Maria Cocco's, who is weeding her garden in a black one-piece bathing suit and straw hat. She sends them to the Groceteria, where Ida directs Marcello to buy espresso, fresh pasta, Arborio rice, cornmeal, fresh basil, oregano leaves, mint, garlic, onions, mushrooms, fresh crusty bread, two types of cheese, dried beans, a Genoa salami, a gallon of olive oil, a small bag of sugar and a half-bushel of tomatoes. Ida pronounces the merchandise "adequate" because the store carries real Italian food, made "back home," not the stuff with Italian names manufactured in New Jersey or Toronto. "I make *penne* for the evening meal," she says.

"You're going to simmer sauce in this heat?"

"Is not hot compared to Italy," answers Ida with a shrug. "Even Venezia is hotter. Always we must eat only good food, yes?"

"Absolutely," agrees Marcello, starting to realize the wisdom of his father's decision. Yes, things seem to be a little distant between Senior and Ida right now, but over time they surely will get used to one other. They say couples in arranged marriages always do. Senior must have *something* going for him; after all, Marcello's mother Sofia married him. And what choice does Ida have? Having bought her a one-way ticket to Canada, it's unlikely Senior could afford to send her home no matter how much she begged, unless he puts himself more deeply into debt to Kowalchuck. Sure, she'll shed a few tears and write some sad letters home, but eventually she'll have a baby or two with Pop, maybe start going to mass again, plump up a little, and before you know it, she'll be just like Angela So-and-So and Maria Cocco, making bitter jokes about husbands they don't care for and spending all their time in the kitchen and the church. After Marcello is ordained, he'll come home to visit, put aside his clerical collar and play road hockey with his little half-brothers, say grace at meals, bless the flat with Latin words and holy water before he leaves. Maybe one day Pop will even be able to afford to move the family off Canal Road into a decent home, if he can save enough to get out of the dirty magazine business. Marcello finds comfort in this dream of domesticity which, deep inside it, holds the hope that he will no longer feel attracted to his father's wife, that he will stop imagining Ida, her white clothing strewn on the floor, straddling him the way Claudia did. He can't get this picture out of his mind. Even if he never acts on his desire, he is flirting with a sin so forbidden, it's almost beyond God's forgiveness. Never mind coveting your neighbour's wife, coveting your father's wife is sin of a Biblical proportion, the kind of stuff they banished you for in the Old Testament.

Despite his lingering sense of guilt, Ida's first morning in Shipman's Corners passes more contentedly than Marcello would have thought possible. Downstairs, Senior mans the store, putting on a show of industry for his bride. As Ida searches in the cupboards for knives and pots, Marcello takes out the Frankenstein hi-fi and his mother's opera records. "Maybe you'd like to listen to some music while you work?"

Ida laughs with delight, looking at the 78s. "Antiquities! Do you have perhaps something more modern? The White Beatles?"

Marcello raises his eyebrows. He's never bought a record of his own. He either listens to his mother's or turns on the radio. But he isn't about to disappoint Ida: God knows Pop's already done enough of that. "I think I know where to borrow one."

At the Hryhorchucks' front screen door, he peers in and knocks. He can see Christie's mother, moving through the back room with a cleaning cloth; there's a smell of lemon wax and cooking with a different assortment of spices than the ones Ida is using. He can hear Engelbert Humperdinck on the stereo, Mrs. Hryhorchuck's favourite.

When she notices him, she comes to the door; she's wearing a bikini, a silver scar on her stomach winking out of her bottoms, a kerchief around her head. She shows no sign of being embarrassed being caught cleaning house half-naked.

"Excuse me, Missus – Christie home?"

It takes a moment for Mrs. H. to decipher what he's asking and to put together an answer: despite living in this country since before Christie was born, her English is almost non-existent. She gestures toward the back of the house: "Girl sit in sun!"

Marcello slips along the outside of the house to the back yard. It isn't a yard at all, but a concrete slab. No one knows why Christie's father cemented over the grass, although there is a rumour going around that he tunneled through their basement to build a bomb shelter and the slab is there to protect against atomic radiation. Christie has always denied this story, saying her father was just tired of mowing the lawn and a buddy of his gave him a good price on the concrete.

He finds not only Christie, but Jane and Judy Donato, poured into brightly coloured Sea Queen bikinis, lying on beach towels to soak in radioactivity from the hazy Niagara sky. Christie's transistor radio blasts:

*Yummy, Yummy, Yummy, I got love in my tummy*
*And I feel like a-lovin you*
*Love, you're such a sweet thing*
*Good enough to eat thing*
*And it's just a-what I'm gonna do...*

The girls nod their heads in time to the music, eyes closed. Standing unseen at the edge of the concrete slab, Marcello gives himself a moment to take in the sight of the girls' bodies slick with baby oil.

"Okay: why'd she marry him?" murmurs Christie lazily.

"Somebody *ruined* her, that's why," answers Jane.

"No, I'll tell you why: she wants Senior's money that he's been hiding all these years," says Judy. "There's a thing a girl can do to a guy that will make him give her *anything* she wants."

"Don't let her tell you," warns Jane. "It's absolutely disgusting."

"Well, you *have* to tell me, now," says Christie.

"Okay, listen up, because I am only going to describe this *once*," Judy says, keeping her voice low. "You pull down the man's pants, then his underpants, then you put his thing in your mouth."

*They're only fifteen years old – where did they learn this stuff?* wonders Marcello, in the shadows with nowhere to hide except back into the house where bikinied Mrs. H. roams with a dust cloth, humming along to *The Green Green Grass of Home*.

"That really is disgusting," admits Christie. "But if your mouth is full, how can you tell him what you want?"

"Maybe you tell him what you want first, *then* do the thing?" suggests Jane.

"Or *after*," says Judy. "You can tell him you'll do it again if he buys you a bottle of perfume, or a new RCA colour console TV, or something."

"How long does it go on?" Christie wants to know. "Are we talking about hours, minutes or seconds?"

Jane makes a gagging sound. "That's a disgusting question."

Judy thinks about it. "Depends on how much he's had to drink and how late he was up playing cards. Five minutes, give or take. Until he goes off."

"Goes off?" says Christie in confusion.

Judy sighs. "You are such a child."

His back to the wall of the house, Marcello finally clears his throat.

The girls look up at him, eyes wide, then glance at each other. "How long you been there, Cello?" asks Christie.

"Not long. Your mom sent me through."

"So! What's happening?"

Marcello shrugs and shoves his hands in his pockets, trying to act casual. "I was just wondering whether maybe you have some records you could loan me? Just for the afternoon."

"Uh...I don't listen to opera."

"I'm not looking for opera. I was thinking maybe the Beatles – the *White Album*, if you have it? Something new."

Christie stands up. "Give me a sec."

She's back in a moment with a stack of LPs. *Revolver. A Hard Day's Night. Help!* And a bunch of others: The Guess Who, The Beach Boys, Dusty Springfield, The Byrds, The Doors, and, improbably, one lonely Tom Jones album.

"Ida likes rock and roll, huh?" says Christie, twisting her hair back off her face.

Marcello shrugs. "Why not?"

"Yeah, right – everybody's mother wants to do the Watusi in the middle of the day," murmurs Judy from her towel.

The other girls laugh as Marcello backs out of the yard, arms full of vinyl.

Marcello takes the albums upstairs and shows them to Ida, who starts playing them one after another. When he goes down to take his place behind the counter of the store, he can hear the music pounding through the floor; when she puts on *A Hard Day's Night*, she cranks up the volume, causing the old wooden building to shake. Pop finally comes out of the storeroom: "What the hell is that noise? Sounds like cats."

"It's Ida, listening to music," explains Marcello.

Senior throws up his hands in disgust. "Better tell her, this place got no breakers. She gonna burn the place down."

"It's okay Pop, I'll let her know not to use the stove and hi-fi at the same time," Marcello reassures him.

At lunchtime, Ida brings down *panini*, made with the good bread she bought that morning, filled with *provolone*, salami and fat slices of tomato, dotted with fresh basil, pepper and dribs of olive oil. Marcello eats at the counter with Ida, who flips through a *Seventeen* magazine while she nibbles at a saucer of carrot sticks. Pop takes his sandwich into the storeroom: *Guiding Light* is on.

Right after lunch, Marcello and Senior start anticipating dinner – *penne* with sauce that Ida spent the day simmering. Senior, amazingly, brings her a bouquet of flowers – a little wilted with more than a few naked stalks, probably from the trash barrel behind Kowalchuck's Flower Shop. Ida makes a show of liking them and puts them in water in a cottage cheese container.

They eat late, after the sun goes down and the flat gets a little cooler. Ida opens a bottle of wine – *where the hell did she get that?* wonders Marcello. When he asks, all she will tell him is that it was a gift from a "young admirer."

On cue, a knock comes at the door. Marcello turns in his seat to the blistered face of Bum Bum, shading his eyes through the screen.

"Ah, speak of devil!" laughs Ida.

"What the hell do you want?" demands Marcello, drawing a surprised glance from Ida.

Bum Bum ignores them both, and looks at Senior. "He said, come get you. He got a poker game up at his mother's and he want to talk to you."

Senior raises his hand in agreement and burps. "Okay, okay, tell him I come." He stands and gives Marcello and Ida a stern women-and-children look.

"Business," he states, with importance. "You two can watch TV, if you want."

Instead, after Senior has trundled across the street to the flower shop, Marcello and Ida take their glasses of wine onto the front stoop and gaze at the full moon hanging luridly over the ships' cranes at the dry docks.

"The Americans will be there in a few weeks. See? That's the Sea of Tranquility, where they'll be landing," Marcello points out.

"I know. Apollo! Like you," smiles Ida. "All you need are a white horse and chariot."

Marcello hopes he can't see the heat of embarrassment rising to his face. He's got to get the hell out of here before he does something for which he'll be damned for all time.

At midnight, Ida goes upstairs and Marcello goes back to the Chevy. He can't sleep.

He stares at the stars through the open window of the car, thinking unhealthy thoughts of Ida. Ida, his stepmother, his father's wife. Filled with self-loathing, he gets up, pulls his clothes back on and crosses the road; the craps game has floated back to the neighbourhood. A light is on in old Mrs. Kowalchuck's flat: Senior must be up there playing cards and 'doing business' right now. *Like father, like son*, reasons Marcello.

Before disappearing down the laneway to join the craps players, he glances up at the window over the candy store. The light is still on there too. He sees Ida in a white night dress, peering down at Canal Road, brushing her hair; must be hotter than hell in there.

He listens to excitement building in the gamblers' voices. Like music, rising to a crescendo when they throw the dice, diminishing when they lose. He wants to play but he'll have to borrow from Stinky again, a bad idea. He turns and heads back to the car. When he glances up at the window of the flat, the light is off. Ida has disappeared.

# 5

KOWALCHUCK, STINKY AND SENIOR are playing straight
sevens and drinking beer in their shirtsleeves. Bum Bum sits
on a bar stool, elbows on knees, back hunched; he's following
the game, ready to take orders for drinks or food or whatever
else they want, the second they want it, or sooner. He's trying
not to show how interested he is in what they are saying about
Senior's bride. The boy loves her. If they ever found out they'd
tease him to death.

The three men are slumped in captain's chairs with padded
leather seats, hearts and swears gouged into the wooden
armrests. The chairs came from a Surf 'N Turf in the Falls;
Kowalchuck made him carry them out of the dark restaurant
to a truck in the middle of the night, then up the stairs to
his mother's place. Even with every window thrown open, the
room is choked with smoke. Kowalchuck keeps mopping his
face with a tea towel so that he won't mark the cards with dribs
of sweat.

"I thought she'd be bigger in the tits and ass department,
like Anita Ekberg," says Kowalchuck, scanning his cards.

"Cute, though," comments Stinky. "And blonde, like
Ekberg."

Kowalchuck shows a seven, followed by an eight. "Yeah
nice blonde hair. No complaint there."

"Possible straight," observes Stinky.

"Smart as a whip," says Senior with a note of pride in his
voice, showing a ten. "And talk! Talk, talk, talk, talk, talk. One
hell of a cook, though. Even better than Junior's mother."

"Pot stinks," says Stinky.

Senior frowns and throws another fifty cents into the
middle of the table.

The boy thinks of the circle of men around the table as a nest, but not a cozy one full of baby birds: an army nest, the kind in a foxhole with machine guns and stuff. Everyone has his special job to do.

Kowalchuck is the General. Stinky is the Lieutenant. Senior is Sarge. Bum Bum is Private Pasquale.

When they still had a TV there was a show he liked. *Combat!* Once there was a GI on the show named Pasquale. He was supposed to be from Brooklyn. This made the boy proud. But by the first commercial Private Pasquale was dead, his friend Littlejohn blasting a German artillery nest with gunfire, yelling: "That's for Pasquale!" At first the boy was disappointed that Private Pasquale was never coming back. But then it didn't matter because the TV itself disappeared along with most of the other stuff in the house, the couch and chairs and dining room table parading out the front door on men's legs, arms and hands wrapped around their tummies, muscles bulging like Popeye's. Bum Bum would have laughed if his Mamma and Nonna hadn't been crying and cursing so loud.

It makes him extra tired to breathe in all the smoke. The men's words are getting hard to understand. They keep saying that Ida belongs to Senior. But while Senior's other girls are shiny, flat and dirty, Ida is all warm skin and not dirty at all. She's like Our Lady. All that nice food! He smelled it through the candy store window. And when big Marcello was stacking boxes in the storeroom, Pasquale brought her a present, a bottle of homemade wine that he bummed off a farmer. Ida was delighted, talking to him like he was a regular kid. She even speaks Italian although she's hard to understand. Her words sound like billiard bills crashing into one another. Some of his Italian words made her laugh, too, but not in a bad way.

He snaps back to attention at the sound of Kowalchuck's raised voice. He's yelling and throwing a newspaper across the table at Senior. "'The state got no business in the bedrooms of the nation' – fuck *me*. First, bootlegging. Now smut. All the government does is get in the way of business," gripes Kowalchuck. "If they legalize everything, who's gonna pay for it?"

Senior strikes a match to light a cigar. "Grocer over Beamsville way still got bust for selling *Playboy* but he say was worth it."

"You're shittin' me," says Stinky.

"No, is true. Business is good," insists Senior indignantly. "Junior say we clear two hundred last week alone."

Kowalchuck pounds a fist on the table, making the cards jump, startling Bum Bum. "Yeah, today, tomorrow, next week, we got customers. For how long? Pretty soon they can get what we got in any corner store, right out in the open. We can't just sit on our asses and expect business to come to us. We got to change with the times."

Bum Bum wants to sleep. Letting his eyes close, just for a minute, he thinks about the toy soldier the fire department brought him last Christmas. GI Joe. He had two different arms, one dark brown, one light brown, but he could still shoot, even though he didn't have a gun anymore. His Nonna said the GI Joe came from some rich kid who broke it and gave it to the fire department who fixed it for poor kids like him so that they would be grateful and kiss the rich folks' asses. Bum Bum took the GI Joe down to the canal and pushed him over the side. "Fuck you, Private Pasquale," he said, but the GI Joe didn't die right away because the shipping season was over and the water level had dropped, the little that was left freezing solid. GI Joe lay on the ice for days until a mid-winter thaw finally sucked him into the drink. The boy kept going back to check. When GI Joe finally disappeared the boy went to the door of the church and put some holy water into his cupped hand, carried it back to the lock and threw it in. "That's for Private Pasquale," he whispered.

Bum Bum comes back to life to a short, sharp whack in the face – nothing too bad, not the kind that would knock out a tooth. Kowalchuck hits Private Pasquale that hard sometimes, to toughen him up. When you're a soldier, you can't be too tough. "Check on my mother," he orders and looks back to his cards.

The boy climbs off the stool and goes to the bedroom. Old Mrs. K. is in a recliner, her swollen legs up on a little stool that jumps out of the chair when you lean back. She's watching an old movie on TV: a bunch of guys sway back and forth with music things in their mouths. There's a vacant blueness to Mrs. K's gaze that makes Bum Bum feel creepy but safe. She's scary but can't hurt him. Her big, soft body fills the recliner like a sack of sugar. When she sees him, she says something in Ukrainian and reaches out to stroke his face. She thinks Bum Bum is her son. The boy pats her hand and goes into the kitchenette to get her a glass of 7-Up.

When Bum Bum comes back into the living room, Senior is scooping the pot toward him with open arms, like the money is his girlfriend. He's won the hand.

Kowalchuck folds his cards and looks across the table: "I'm going to speak plain to you, Senior: I don't think you're good for what you owe me for Ida."

Stacking his chips into piles, Senior looks up at Kowalchuck in surprise: "We take it out of our profits, we shake on it."

Kowalchuck waves his hand at the front page of the newspaper again. "That was *before*. Not now that Mr. Pisspot E. Trudeau put us out of business."

"Commie asshole," observes Stinky.

"The Bank of Kowalchuck's calling your loan. You got one week to settle your debt to me. More than generous."

Senior drops his cigar on the floor. Bum Bum jumps down to pick it up but Stinky gives him a warning look. He climbs back on the stool and tries to turn invisible.

"Come on Glen. You know I ain't got it," Senior says. "You pissed 'cause I won the hand?"

Kowalchuck moves into the captain's chair one over from Senior and puts his hand on his shoulder. The hair stands up on the back of Bum Bum's neck just watching him. "I'm thinking about giving up the magazine business. The future's in movies now. Maybe Ida could do some modeling for us."

Now Senior seems really unhappy. Bum Bum can tell by the way his mouth hangs open a little bit and his hands shake and his eyes don't look at nobody.

After a while, Senior says: "She's my wife. Get the girls at the pool hall to do it. They're used to it."

"I want a blonde. And what the hell, I paid for her. Why shouldn't I get first dibs?" Kowalchuck stretches. "After I'm finished, you can have her back."

Senior gets up from the table. Bum Bum can see sweat running from under his tangle of grey hair, down the neck of his shirt. There's a big wet blotch between his shoulder blades.

"You don't put a hand on her," he says.

"You got another idea?" asks Kowalchuck.

Bum Bum knows. He grips his hands, one in another. *Please please please please please. Don't let them touch Our Lady,* he prays. If they start playing with her, she'll go dead inside. She won't cook no more.

Senior stares at the chips. Not looking up, he says: "The only other thing I got is the store."

Bum Bum can tell by the fat smile on Kowalchuck's face that this is what he really wants, or wants at least as much as he does Ida. *The store.* He's heard him tell Stinky about how he could really make something out of the place, instead of just letting it go to hell the way Senior does. *Real estate, that's the future, you think this lousy neighbourhood's gonna stay rundown forever? One day some smart developer's gonna put a strip mall in and guess who he's gonna have to talk to.*

But Kowalchuck never says what he thinks, not right away.

"Store's not worth enough," he tells Senior. Then, as if in answer to Bum Bum's prayer, he opens his mouth in a different kind of smile, showing all his teeth at once. "'Course, there's always Junior. Throw him in too and we could have a deal."

**6**

*July 3*

MORNING DAWNS HOT AND bright. Everyone is complaining about the lack of rain but Marcello is grateful to be able to sleep in the car with the windows open without getting soaked. Lying on the back seat of the Chevy, he can feel the humidity already starting to build. It's going to be another scorcher.

"*Marcello! Vieni qua!*"

He hears his name called from a window at the back of the flat, directly above him. Looking up, he sees Ida, hair pulled back in a ponytail, sticking her head out to call down to him.

"Do you smell it?" she calls out.

"Smell what?"

She laughs. "Good coffee! Come and taste!" Then disappears inside the flat.

Marcello gets out of the car and, with a glance upwards to make sure he can't be seen in his underwear, pulls on his jeans. He's going to have to get a fresh set of clothes soon; either that or take a blanket to the coin laundry and wrap himself in it while these ones go through the wash. Damp tee shirts carpet the floor of the Chevy.

He goes around to the fire escape to climb up to the flat and is surprised to see Bum Bum sitting on the lowest step with a cup of milky coffee and a slab of buttered toast.

"Your mamma is nice," he says, mouth full.

"What are you doing here?"

"I hear she want good food. So I bum a basket of strawberries and some wine for her."

Marcello's eyes narrow suspiciously. "Who from?"

"Farmer from other side of canal. Swap him for a few fingers of rye left in the bottle last night."

To his amazement, Ida appears at the top of the stairs, coffee pot in hand. "More *café con leche*, Pasquale?"

Bum Bum grins and lifts his cup. As Ida pours, Marcello looks at her and slowly shakes his head. She looks him straight in the eye and lifts an eyebrow inquiringly. *Che?*

Later, when they're alone together in the flat, he tries to explain things to her. "The boy's a moocher. A scrounger and a snitch. A mental defective. Other things, too, even worse. A thief, a beggar. His mother's a beggar too. An awful family. Outcasts. And Ida, I don't know how to put this – Bum Bum goes with perverts. For money. Understand?"

Ida puts a hand on her mouth, wrinkles her forehead and studies Marcello's face.

"Pasquale is just a child. You think he does not deserve our pity with such a life?"

Marcello rubs his face with both hands: why does she have to make so much damn sense? "Yeah, yeah, I guess so. Just be careful around him. He's sneaky. You give him food and coffee and he'll never let you alone."

Ida frowns and turns her back on Marcello. "You want to 'help people', you tell me, but you have no room in your heart for this child. I did not imagine you as such a cruel man, Cello."

"Me? Cruel?" He almost points out that everyone is cruel to Bum Bum, that he was put on this earth to invite abuse, but realizes that this will only anger Ida more. She doesn't understand rough-edged neighbourhoods like this one or the awfulness of Bum Bum's life. Who would want the kid around? Or risk being nice to him? Although she did make a stinging point about the vow he is supposed to be taking to help the least of God's children. He sighs.

"*Mi dispiace*, Ida. I'm sorry, you're right, the boy deserves our charity, I guess."

"And our love too I think. *All* children deserve love," replies Ida hoarsely and turns her back on him, busying herself with nothing special at the counter.

Marcello walks over to Angela So-and-So's house, where he finds her watering the lawn, and asks for a few roses from her front garden. When Marcello brings the peace offering to Ida, she accepts the flowers in silence, placing them in the cottage cheese container with the naked stalks of Senior's trashbarrel bouquet. The two don't speak to one another for the rest of the morning. Her silence leaves Marcello feeling hollow. He can sense the void once again, just outside the candy store door, waiting to slip in.

Marcello and Ida are still avoiding one another when Senior shuffles into the store in his ill-fitting suit, looking weary. *Probably a hangover*, thinks Marcello. He watches his father put an arm around Ida to kiss her on the cheek and say a few words that he can't make out.

Senior jerks his head at Marcello. "Need to talk private business, Junior."

Inside the storeroom, Senior closes the door and sits heavily on the cot, his eyes pouchy and tired-looking. Like Marcello, he must be having sleeping problems.

"Kowalchuck got a job for you, Junior. Some big shot business, out in the country."

Marcello shakes his head. "Pop, I'm going to the seminary, soon as Father can arrange it. But I've got to start living clean. You understand?"

Senior sighs, hands on knees; he's avoiding Marcello's eyes.

"You do this job. Out of respect to me, your father, who has cared for you all these years. Out of respect for your stepmother Ida. *Capisci?*"

Marcello feels the familiar damp itchy warmth spreading across his chest. A warning. He crosses his arms.

"I don't think so, Pop. Kowalchuck's job could land me in jail. You too."

Senior lifts his hands in a *no discussion* gesture.

"You doing it," he says flatly. "I go to Lewiston now for two days with Kowalchuck and his mother. When we back, you do the job. That's all there is to it."

Without waiting for Marcello to respond, he leaves the storeroom, tossing a *ciao* to Ida as he passes through the store.

The rest of the day unfolds with the monotony of Gregorian Chant. Marcello pulls out the Cheer box, again and again, conscious of Ida watching him from where she sweeps the floor and dusts the shelves. After he sells a heavy Dutch issue to a blonde sailor who's come down from the canal, Ida says: "I should learn this part of your father's business."

Marcello looks at her in surprise. "They're men's magazines, Ida. Not something you should touch."

She shrugs indifferently. "I have seen these periodicals before. Very popular, back home. Once you go to the priests, this will be my job, yes?"

"That's up to Pop," answers Marcello curtly, but he's sure that Senior would never let Ida touch the Cheer box; what decent woman would want to?

"Of course. Always, my life is up to someone else," she mutters, picking up a copy of *Photoplay* and paging through it restlessly. As he shoves the box back under the counter and closes the top, Marcello tries to makes sense of Ida. Sometimes she reminds him of a little white nun, bustling around in her bleached-out clothing, cooking and preaching at him about needy children; other times, she seems a little too worldly for his liking. He's tempted to ask if her proxy vow included to love and obey.

Does she love Senior? (*Doubt it.*) Will she obey him? (*When it suits her.*) And now she isn't even speaking to Marcello. (*What the hell did I say?*) He decides to get out his chessboard and set up a game against himself on the counter.

Hunched over the board, he's a couple of moves in when he becomes conscious that Ida is beside him. Watching him.

"You know chess?"

Ida shakes her head.

"Want to learn?"

She nods. "Yeah-sure-okay!"

Marcello starts to run through the rules but it's quickly obvious that Ida has no aptitude or interest in the game. She seems to find the board interesting, though. She stands at the counter, repeating the names of the pieces over and over again, as if committing them to memory: Queen, King, Rook, Bishop, Knight, Pawn.

"A rook is a castle? I think it is a bird."

Marcello shrugs. "I'm not sure why they call it that."

"And what is a pawn?" she asks, picking one up.

"Something…powerless. Something totally controlled by others. A person can be a pawn."

"Ah." Ida quickly puts the piece back on the board and picks up the Queen. "I like this one best. Very powerful. She goes where she wants to go."

That night, when Marcello walks out to the Chevy, he hears music. "Nowhere Man." Someone is in the front seat, playing the radio. When he pulls open the front door, trying to surprise whoever is there, Marcello finds Bum Bum sprawled out, reading an old copy of *I, Robot* that Marcello stole from his high school library. The kid's holding the book upside-down.

"What's this say?" asks Bum Bum turning the book toward Marcello.

Marcello sighs. "Didn't you ever learn to read?"

Bum Bum, shrugs and sits up. "Yeah. Just not so many words."

Normally the sight of the boy handling his things would have filled Marcello with disgust, but he's got other things on his mind. "Switch off the radio. You're going to drain the battery."

Bum Bum turns off the song in mid-chorus and looks at Marcello expectantly.

Marcello takes the book, opens the back door and sits half in, half out of the car. He remembers Ida's lecture about the importance of kindness and understanding, about being nice to the kid.

"It's a book of stories about robots. In the future, robots are almost like people, very advanced. Like a species of their own."

He suspects that Bum Bum has no idea what he's talking about. He stares at Marcello over the back of the seat. "Read me."

Marcello sighs. What the hell. "Okay. One story, then you go to sleep. The first one's called "Robbie." *'Ninety-eight, ninety-nine, one hundred'. Gloria withdrew her chubby little forearm from before her eyes...'*"

By the time Marcello finishes "Robbie," it's too dark to read; he asks Bum Bum to hand him the flashlight in the glove. He's only two pages into the next story when he hears the sound of slow, steady breathing. He peers over the seat and sees Bum Bum curled up, the knob of one knee resting against the stick shift.

Marcello lies back and switches off the flashlight. He listens to Bum Bum's baby-breathing and the creaking of the cicada – isn't this heat wave ever going to break?

Sleep won't come. Finally he pushes open the door and walks around to the front of the store. The flat light is still on. Grateful for this small mercy, he climbs the fire escape and peers through the screen door.

In her thin white nightgown, Ida is curled up on the old couch, feet tucked under her like a bird in a nest; she's reading a *Vogue* that was accidentally delivered to the store with the regular order of *Tiger Beat*. Music plays softly, his mother's old recording of Mario Lanza singing "Nessun Dorma," while a small metal fan pushes the damp air around the flat. Marcello is suddenly suspicious that the fan was a gift from Bum Bum, probably something he scrounged from someone's garbage; he can't imagine Pop springing for it. Marcello is annoyed that he didn't think of finding one for Ida himself in the junk shop.

He knocks lightly on the doorframe, not wanting to barge in. Ida looks up, startled; when she sees that it's him, she visibly relaxes. "Cello! Come in!"

Marcello stands in the doorway. "I read Pasquale a bedtime story. Now I can't sleep. Can I sit with you for a while?"

"*Certo!*" She pats the couch cushion beside her, then jumps up. "I make you a chamomile."

"Don't trouble yourself," he murmurs, watching her bustle around finding a pot and lighting the stove, *tsking* when a burner refuses to light.

"*Ma che*, this stove," she complains, shaking her head.

"I'll fix it for you," he promises, taking a seat on the couch. "Maybe I'll even get the kid to help me. Wouldn't hurt him to learn something useful." He glances at the page she was looking at in *Vogue*. "What Your Stars Forecast for July 1969."

"Horoscopes. You don't believe in religion, but you believe in this stuff?"

"*Pfff.* Is just for fun. I am born on May fifteen. *Toro* the Bull. A stubborn sign."

"So, you just had a birthday not long ago. How old did you turn?"

Ida looks at him, shaking her head in non-comprehension. "I turn something?"

"It just means, how old did you become?"

She hesitates, then says: "I have twenty-four years."

Marcello laughs and shakes his head. Ida raises her eyebrows. "My birthday is comical?"

He nods. "Pop said you were thirty-four."

Ida stares at Marcello in horror. "I look so old?"

"No, you don't. That's why I asked."

Ida takes her place on the couch beside him, handing him the mug of tea. "What is your star sign, Cello?"

"No idea. My birthday's January ninth."

"Then you are *Capricorno*. A very intelligent, practical sign. This sounds like you. Read your future to me."

Marcello runs his finger down the page, finding Capricorn the Goat: "'Life holds many surprises large and small this month'." He looks up at Ida. "There's one down in the Chevy right now. Unfortunately."

Ida laughs. "Kindness to an unwanted child will get you into heaven." She curls up beside him, feet tucked under, as she watches him sip his tea; he can taste that she's added a dollop of honey. She pulls the *Vogue* from the couch and tosses it to the floor, swinging her feet between her and Marcello, her white gown tugged tight at the knees; Marcello can see a necklace of perspiration on the lace piping on her chest, the tiny buds of her nipples underneath.

"Does something trouble your mind so that you cannot sleep?" she asks.

He looks at her over the rim of the mug. "No, just the heat," he lies. Summoning courage, he brings himself to ask a question that has bothered him since the day he first met her: "Ida, I don't understand why a woman like you would marry Pop without even meeting him. Was it really just that stupid story about the horses? I'm thinking there had to be some other reason to leave your family."

"I leave Italy *because* of my family."

She offers this piece of information in a quiet voice, then presses her lips tightly together, as if unwilling to share anything else about herself.

"I'm surprised your father didn't come after you," he presses.

Ida looks into her cup. "My father was dead before I was born, a Partisan in the Garibaldi Brigade. Shot by the Germans in the War."

"A war hero," says Marcello, mildly impressed.

Ida gives a stiff nod of her head. "*Si.* My mamma and I live alone, always."

"You mean, alone with your brother Rico and your *nonna* and *nonno*."

Ida pause. "*Certo*, with them all. This goes without saying."

The two sit side by side, Ida staring at the floor.

Finally he says, "I'm sorry if I'm out of line asking all these questions. You just don't seem to belong in a place like Shipman's Corners."

"I do not belong in many places," she says, still not looking at him.

Marcello listens to the frenzied buzz of the cicada, the teacup cooling in his hands. He stands, sensing that she doesn't want to talk anymore.

"Thanks for the tea, Ida. I'd better get to bed."

As he lets the screen door fall shut behind him, Ida doesn't wish him good night.

With Bum Bum taking over the Chevy, Marcello feels homeless. Tomorrow he's going to have to make it clear to the boy that this was a one-time-only deal; the smell of Bum Bum's unwashed body in the tin can of a car is more than Marcello can handle.

For tonight he'll need to bunk out somewhere else. He walks along the road leading to the canal and scrambles up the embankment. Light stands illuminate the bollards dotting the waterway but further inland there are patches of ground in shadow. He finds a dark spot, lies on his back, says a distracted *Our Father*, then stares up at the night sky, looking for constellations. Stargazing always gives him a sensation similar to going to High Mass or listening to certain types of music – Beethoven, Thomas Tallis – as though he's touching something huge and deep and unchanging and mysterious, vastly larger than himself. He gets a painful comfort knowing his suffering doesn't matter at all in the grand scheme of the universe.

He wonders if the Moon knows the lengths men are prepared to go to be first to touch her. Is she aware that three Americans will soon be hurtling toward her surface, determined to mount her or die? Will she embrace them or see their coming as a violation? *Stupid, stupid*, he tells himself: *the Moon doesn't have feelings, it's just a pale hunk of frozen rock in the sky. Stop anthropomorphizing.*

Dreamily, he starts piecing together the stars – the Bull, the Goat, the Seated Woman – until, without thinking about it, he drops off to sleep.

# 7

MARCELLO CROUCHES ON THE floor of the flat, *Gianni Schicchi* on the Frankenstein hi-fi, a junkyard of electrical parts scattered around him. The ancient Moffat stove is throwing up its secrets. He told Ida he would fix the stove, and it's one promise he can happily make good on.

For Marcello, a malfunctioning machine is a puzzle to be solved, finding and fixing what ails it, an adventure. He can see the source of the trouble and, no surprise, it's corrosion. Wire cutters and screwdriver in hand, the stove tipped precariously on its side, he tries to look up into the yawning socket of the burner opening. It's hard to maneuver in the space because the stove and fridge have been jerry-rigged into an alcove. The flat was never meant for human habitation, thinks Marcello: it's just a glorified attic.

"Pasquale, you're skinnier than me, get in there and tell me what you see."

His assistant wriggles under the listing edge of the stove and peers inside the burner hole, crusty with the residue of years of boiled-over tinned soup.

"Rust," he pronounces.

"What else?"

"Wires. Thick black ones."

"Any of them look worn? As if they've been scorched or scraped?"

"All of them. One is a sort of unravel, like when the bottom of your jeans come apart," he reports.

"Good description. We'll need to replace that," explains Marcello.

He spreads tools on the floor between them. "There's money in small appliance repair. That'd be a good trade for you."

The boy taps his head. "Too stupid. That what my Pop say."

"Yeah, well, he's wrong. You catch onto things quick."

Through the floor grate, they can hear an off-key rendering of "Raindrops Keep Falling on My Head": Ida, singing her heart out at the candy counter. Marcello winces slightly; she may have an ear for languages but none for music.

Bum Bum spools up a length of wire. The kid isn't the mental defective Marcello once believed him to be. He's actually a quick learner, if you show him what to do. He's even picked up chess. But something is still 'off' in other ways, like not being able to read. Marcello has tried to teach him, working their way word by word through *I, Robot*, with little success. The kid keeps scrambling up letters, as if he sees them backwards in a mirror. Marcello wishes he could get inside the machinery of the boy's head and figure out what's short-circuiting there.

Bum Bum looks over at the grate again, scratching at his scalp. "I heard Ida's having a honeymoon for now, but after that, the real work start."

Marcello sits back on his heels, a Robertson screwdriver dangling from one hand. "*Real* work? What do you mean?"

To Marcello's surprise, Bum Bum's ravaged face pinks up: he's blushing. "You know, dirty-girl stuff." To demonstrate, he jiggles his hands up and down in front of his chest. "If someone try to hurt her, I kill them."

Marcello sets down his hammer, shocked (and a little jealous) of Bum Bum's protectiveness toward Ida. "Don't be stupid, Pasquale, Pop would never let her do that kind of stuff. And no one's going to kill anyone, except me you if you don't keep working."

With the stove's guts disgorged on the floor, Marcello and Bum Bum head down the fire escape to the candy store. It's quiet today. Ida sits on a stool reading *Seventeen*. She's abandoned her skirt and white blouse today in favour of denim cut-offs and a tee shirt, her hair pinned up messily; at first glance you might think one of the neighbourhood schoolgirls was working at the counter. "How goes?" she asks.

"We're going to need a few bucks for parts." Digging into the cash register, Marcello pulls multicoloured bills out from under the drawer. Ida peers at them: "What type of money is this? *La Regina Elisabetta* has been replaced with *uno vecchio Scozzese.*"

"Canadian Tire money. The old Scotsman shows you can shop there cheaply. He's, how you say – a thrifty Scot."

Ida laughs. "Like you. Thrifty and practical. You're an Old Scotsman yourself, Cello."

Marcello takes the bills from her hand. "I've been called worse."

The drive across the bridge into the 'good part' of Shipman's Corners takes ten minutes but feels like travelling into an alternate universe in one of Marcello's sci-fi novels. On the other side of the canal, subdivisions are being carved out of what until recently were peach orchards stretching off to the horizon; the sprawling Canadian Tire is part of a new shopping plaza built to serve families in the aluminum-sided split levels with their carports and basketball hoops and anemic gardens. Marcello misses the sugary scent of ripening peaches that used to fill the air but he likes Canadian Tire too. The store is a cathedral of gleaming hardware and sports gear, heady with the off-gassing of rubber, vinyl and plastic polymers.

Lost in the sea of bicycles and camping equipment, Bum Bum reaches out to touch the streamers on the handle of a CCM Mustang bike, lime green with fat white-walled tires. He trails Marcello from aisle to aisle as they pick up wire, burner rings and a soldering iron. The Canadian Tire money saves Marcello $2.53 at the cash. He buys a small metal tape measure with the savings and presents it to Bum Bum as a gift: "To be a handyman, you've got to have your own tools." On the way home, the boy extends the tape and watches it zip back into its case over and over again.

It only takes a couple of hours to get the stove in working order. By lunchtime all four burners are heating.

"Houston, we have lift off," announces Marcello, wiping grease from his hands with a tea towel. He offers his hand to Bum Bum who wrinkles his face in suspicion: "Why you want to touch me?"

"Men usually shake hands after they do a little good honest work together," Marcello explains.

Bum Bum grabs his hand and shakes, gripping as hard as he can. Then he puts his face to the floor grate and shouts down, "Stove's working!"

Ida's voice floats up: "*Bravo*! I come up and make us lunch. Pasquale, could you watch the store?"

Bum Bum looks at Marcello in surprise; he's never been entrusted at the counter before.

"Go ahead," nods Marcello. "Just don't let me catch you stealing anything or I'll break your arms."

Ida's excitement is palpable as she runs up the fire escape to the flat; the stove with its new burners has been pushed back against the wall and the floor swept clean, as if the repairs had simply occurred by magic.

"I really not think you able to do this, you know," she admits, shaking her head. "Once again I am in your debt, Cello."

"It's nothing. I enjoy fixing things."

"All same, thank you," she says, and touches his hand, her fingers chilly despite the heat of the day.

Marcello tries to turn his attention to gathering his tools but is uncomfortably aware that Ida is standing close to him. His nose is full of the cooking smells that cling to her clothing – oregano, basil and oil. When he looks at her, she places her hands on his face.

*Just kiss her*, a tiny scrap of Marcello's brain insists before it winks out like a busted picture tube. Leaning down, he brushes his lips against Ida's forehead and her cheeks. The edge of her ear. Her neck, here and there. Finally, her mouth. Ida kisses him back, her hands touching his face, his hair, his shoulders. His ears are full of the rhythms of baroque horns and drums, as if she is exhaling music into him. He is breaking at least three Commandments, yet feels peaceful for a change.

His embrace is so tight that Ida's feet leave the floor; she wraps her legs around his waist, her arms around his neck. His body feels like a tree growing into hers, entwined in the eye of an invisible storm. Cradling her bottom, he gives her a little boost to secure his hold. Her lightness makes him feel strong and he sways gently from side to side in time to silent music. *Maybe we can stand like this forever*, he thinks.

Ida draws her face back, her hand toying with the curls at Marcello's neck.

"*Voglio fare l'amore con te*," she tells him.

*Did she just say that she wants to make love with me?* Marcello searches her face for some sign that he's misunderstood.

"Are you sure, Ida?"

She leans her forehead against his, and says: "*Si. Subito.*" *Yes. Right now.*

Marcello carries her to the bedroom and spreads her on the mattress, the counterpane ruched up beneath her like the waves of a blue satin sea. Kneeling over her, he tugs off her shirt and unclips the back of her white bra. She helps Marcello pull his oily tee shirt off over his head. Her eyes widen at the sight of the red scratches on his chest as he lowers himself onto her, the crucifix around his neck dancing between her breasts.

The dresser mirror reflects their bodies in its crazed surface, Marcello's tanned deep brown and covered in coarse black hair, Ida's so pink and smooth she looks like she would melt away in sunlight. They are like two different species of animal, not human beings born in the same part of the world.

Ida runs her hand down the track of black hair on Marcello's belly into the top of his jeans, drawing a gasp out of him.

A puddle of clothes collects on the floor. Ida takes Marcello's hand and places it between her legs. Not sure what to do, he lets Ida guide him, her hand on his.

He wants to slow down but his cock bumps blindly on Ida's belly. He can't wait any longer. And she wants him, doesn't she? He nudges her legs open with his thigh and enters her. Something gives way. He hears Ida's distant voice and the pressure of her hands against his aching chest.

In a spurt and a shout, it's over. As he floats from ecstasy to drowsiness, he realizes that Ida is crying. Despite that initial blaze of passion, something is wrong. He rolls off and sees a smear of blood across her thighs and his. Gathering her up, he says: "Did I hurt you?"

"A bit," she says quietly. "I didn't think it would be painful."

Marcello cradles her, *shooshing* her and rubbing her back and going *now now now*, until she whispers that she needs the bathroom.

Arms and legs flung wide, half-drunk cock bobbing, he lets the humid air blanket his muscles as he listens to water running and imagines Ida with a cloth, washing herself where he's just been. He notices a bloodstain on the counterpane and touches it with his fingers; it's still wet. The sight is strangely satisfying. *She was a virgin*, he thinks happily, although a thought briefly intrudes that women bleed for other reasons.

When Ida returns to the bedroom, her little breasts peeking at Marcello from under her robe, she curls up next to him. He feels himself hardening but his conscience is stiffening too. "We can never do this again," he makes himself say.

"*Perche non?* We can run away together. Don't you love me?"

"Of course I love you, Ida. But run away? I haven't got a cent to my name. How would we get by? Where would we go?"

"*Pfff!* We go to Toronto, to New York, to the Moon! *Non importa.* I go with you anywhere, Cello. As for money, there is at least two hundred in the till downstairs."

Marcello brushes his hand against her nipples, feeling them harden. He can't believe she's letting him do this, or how beautiful she is. He could lie here looking at her naked little body all day. He wants to make love to her again. Instead he says: "You belong to my father."

"Cello," she says, her voice shaking, "I belong to no one at all except myself. Certainly not your father. Not even you. I am free."

For reasons he doesn't understand himself, Marcello feels a surge of anger: "*Free?* Then why the hell did you marry a man you'd never even met? What was that all about?"

"That was about your father's deception. You and me start over."

He sits up. "Let's say I steal Pop's money. How far do you think we'll get before we're caught? He'll send the cops after us, Ida. He'll say I robbed him and kidnapped you."

Ida sits up and states something that she must have been thinking about for some time: "Your father is Marcello Trovato. You also are Marcello Trovato. Who is to say which one I marry?"

"It's Pop's signature on the papers, not mine," he points out.

Ida puts her face in her hands. "If this were Italian opera, you would find a way."

Marcello shakes his head. "This isn't Italy, Ida. It isn't opera. This is real life in Canada. We have to be practical here."

"*Ma che cosa dici?*" says Ida bitterly. "Ah, I forgot! You are a *vecchio Scozzese*, not an Italian man."

She rolls away, her bathrobe a white wall. He reaches for her, trying to get her to face him.

"Ida," he says, and she turns to him, finally. Already, his cock is betraying him. No matter how scraped raw his conscience feels, his body insists on re-entry.

He pushes into her so suddenly this time that the pleasure is like an explosion for him – for her too, he thinks. No cry of pain this time, just wetness and warmth. When it's over, Ida slides off him and closes her eyes.

"*Ho sonno,*" she yawns and touches his lips with her cold fingertips.

"Sleep awhile," he says.

He suddenly remembers Pasquale downstairs. Pop will be back soon and he doesn't want him to see the boy manning the counter. Or find his son in bed with his wife.

Picking his jeans off the floor, he watches Ida doze. He leaves her bed, telling himself *never again.*

## 8

WITH IDA AND MARCELLO not speaking or looking at one another, even Senior notices the cold silence in the candy store. When Marcello fails to show up in the flat for the evening meal, his father approaches him. "You two have a fight or something, Junior?"

"No, just – you know, I got things on my mind."

"Me too. Kowalchuck's job," frowns Senior. "You in, right?"

"Come on, Pop, you already know my answer," says Marcello and bangs his way out of the screen door. He can feel Ida's eyes following him. With the countdown to her honeymoon growing shorter, he wonders when Senior will make his way up the fire escape and pull back the blue counterpane on the bed to claim his rights.

Marcello walks to St. Dismas and sits in a back pew of the empty church, listening to the organist practice Pachelbel's "Canon." Normally he finds the piece boring, but today the steady progression of major chords suggests the existence of a peaceable, predictable world, full of happy children, kindly fathers and mothers baking chocolate cakes: no wonder people like Pachelbel at their weddings. Too early for confession, he attempts a decade of the rosary but his mind keeps slipping into thoughts of Ida gazing up at him, lips swollen and mouth open, her hands on his chest as he thrusts. He looks up at the crucified Christ over the altar, reminding himself that sometimes a guy has to make sacrifices.

But by the following evening, with Senior at poker, Marcello can stand the silence no longer and catches her hand as she walks past with a broom: "Can I talk to you in the Chevy tonight?"

The meeting starts as a simple conversation, Marcello trying to explain his duty to his father and his childhood promise to Prima to enter the priesthood. Ida sits quietly and listens, hands folded in the lap of her apron, glancing out the window. No smiles from her now, just a cold anger or something like it: frustration, disappointment, impatience. It's hard to tell with Ida. Marcello's speech ends with "Well, what do you think?"

Ida reaches over and touches the skin of his burning chest with a cold fingertip, between his gold crucifix and the top button of his shirt. "What a strange thing, to carry a tortured man on your chest," she observes.

That's all it takes to reignite Marcello. He pushes her down on the seat and starts kissing her, but knows they can't chance making love in the alley, even after dark: Bum Bum thinks of the Chevy as his second home, a safe place to sleep or hear a story. Marcello drives them out to a farm road where the only light comes from the moon. Parked on a grassy verge next to a vast strawberry field, he refuses to waste time moving into the back seat – precious seconds ticking past – and so opens his jeans and pulls Ida into his lap with a groan. He comes with her mouth on his chest.

"We should drive back," he suggests weakly.

Ida shakes her head. "Not yet," she says. He can see her licking flecks of his blood from her lips. That's when they switch to the back seat, its vinyl-covered expanse making it easier to explore one another.

Wrapped around Ida, Marcello drops off to sleep, awakening a while later to find himself alone. Looking through the open window of the car, he can see the silhouette of her body in moonlight. Arms stretched toward the sky, she's standing at the edge of the drainage ditch, looking toward the endless strawberry fields. Marcello gets out of the car to bring her back before someone sees her – *for God's sake, get in the car, Ida* – but she pulls him to her, skin against skin. With his feet in a puddle of ditchwater, he hoists Ida around him and they make love standing up, Marcello feeling like they are the only man and woman under the Moon, when something slithers over his foot. Looking down he feels rather than sees movement in the high grass of the ditch.

"Be careful, Ida, there's something down there," he warns, setting her on her feet.

Hands cupping her breasts, she glances down. "Is only a snake," she tells him.

Marcello drives back into town at dawn, hoping no one will notice Ida's ascent up the fire escape. "We've got to make sure we come home in the dark next time," he remarks and Ida nods, saying nothing about how *never again* has changed to *next time*. She seems as distracted as he is. He notices something else about her: her breasts are swollen.

He mentions this change to her and worries it's an early sign of pregnancy – he's been trying to pull out of her in time, but knows it isn't a surefire method. She explains that she is just sore from all the touching and sucking and biting; if Marcello's hands aren't on her, then his lips are, his teeth teasing out her nipples. He wonders aloud if it wouldn't be safer to make love between her breasts than between her legs. Ida sighs at this, takes his hand and pushes his fingers inside her; she begs him to try but they don't get far, Marcello eventually enters her in his usual way, his hand over her mouth as she bites down on his fingers to muffle her screams. They don't want farmers hearing them, peering in at them, knocking at the Chevy's windows.

Each long day stretches agonizingly ahead of him, another day of watching Ida move languidly about the store, the body he now thinks of as his, hidden under dresses and aprons. He spends the day waiting for nightfall. When he isn't making love to her, he's thinking about it.

Neither of them is getting any sleep. Marcello groggily stocks shelves in slow motion as Ida dreamily makes change at the counter. The proximity to her body is too much for him and he finds himself going upstairs to the bathroom from time to time to relieve the tension, one hand braced against the wall, the other on his cock, Ida's name in his mouth.

*I'm a mess*, he thinks, looking at himself in a mirror, blood lines lazily tracing their way down his chest like paint drips on a wall. Afraid to sit with Ida and Senior at meals, he is starting to lose weight, his jeans already sagging on his hips. He uses the word *love* to describe what he feels but it's more like obsession; Ida is beginning to spark in him the risky buzz of the craps games. He's always taking things too far, always searching for that peak moment – but unlike gambling, the lovemaking (or call it what it is, the fucking) is one peak moment after another, like winning on every roll. He can barely stand it.

On the candy counter, a romantic display appears out of nowhere: a dozen red roses in a cut glass vase and a dignified gold box with a velvet bow. Marcello glances at the fancy scroll lettering on the box: *Pot of Gold Premium Selection.* Ida is behind the counter, reading a pup tent of a card.

"From your father," she says blandly, her eyes not meeting Marcello's. "He say is to celebrate our life together. Very romantic, no?"

Marcello flips open the box lid. Inside, a chart identifies the vast selection of chocolates, each one completely different from the other. *Chocolate fondue crunch. Caramel swirl. White nougat.* Every name promises pleasure.

"Perhaps your father has more to offer than I thought," muses Ida, examining her choices.

"What do you mean?" demands Marcello.

"At least he declares what he wants. *Beh!* Which to choose?" sighs Ida, picking out a shell-shaped dark chocolate streaked with pink.

"Stop it," says Marcello. If he opened his shirt, he's sure he'd see his skin pierced by thorns, his chest in flames.

A vision enters his head: Senior, on the floor, a red pool spreading beneath him, Pot of Gold chocolates scattered on his crushed and broken body. He remembers the baseball bat behind the counter.

*Get the hell out of here*, Marcello orders himself.

Without speaking to Ida, he leaves the store, gets in the Chevy and drives. Soon he's raising a contrail of dust on a concession road, crossing farm lanes where he and Ida have been making love in the night. He averts his eyes and keeps moving.

As he nears the American border, the farms give way to half-hearted towns. Fort Erie greets him with a collection of Chinese take-outs and rundown souvenir shops, *Buffalo Evening News* paper boxes, tourist rooms and a few taverns. One place, *La Castile*, is done up as a fake castle, the windows blacked out and set with iron bars like a dungeon. Atop a stone cornice chiselled with the words KING EDWARD, a billboard blares STEAKS CHOPS SPAGHETTI COCKTAILS AIR-CONDITIONED GIRLS GIRLS GIRLS! He ponders what air-conditioned girls look like.

Dead ahead, the feminine curve of the Peace Bridge thrusts upward like a Cheer girl in ecstasy; at the top of the arch, the Stars and Stripes snap in the wind alongside the red and white Canadian maple leaf, marking the spot where one country somersaults into the other. Across the rapids, Buffalo stands as square as an Erector set, as pushy and American as a U.S. dollar bill. Marcello swings the Chevy into the lane marked TO USA and pulls up to the booth where a bored-looking U.S. Customs Officer sits waiting, beefy arms crossed.

"Citizenship?"

"Canadian."

"Where do you live?"

"Shipman's Corners."

Something about Marcello's answers causes the officer to hesitate and ask: "Where were you born?"

"Italy."

"Thought I heard an accent. Let's see your naturalization papers."

Marcello looks at the officer helplessly. "Look, sir: I want to enlist in the Marines. To fight in Vietnam."

He expects the man to shake his hand and say something like: *I admire your spirit, son*, but his face is unyielding.

"Vietnam, huh? That's a good one. We've had Canadians coming through here in droves, hitchhiking to that hippie festival in the Catskills. But you need papers. Otherwise I can't let you through. Better listen to it on the radio, kid."

Marcello turns the Chevy away from the border, driving back under the steel claws of the superstructure that grips the rock of the gorge. *You tried*, he tells himself. But the border guard's words keep echoing back to him, heavy with meaning: *You need papers.*

By the time he's reached Shipman's Corners, he has an inspiration. Leaving the Chevy in the parking lot of St. Dismas, he knocks on the rectory door, asking the housekeeper for a word with Father Ray.

The priest comes to the door in shorts and a soccer jersey, dressed to coach a game. "Marcello," he says, extending a hand. "I guess you're checking on that letter to the Passionists. I mailed it out last week."

For a moment, Marcello doesn't know what the priest is talking about. Then, remembering his request for early entry to the seminary, he thanks him and changes the subject: "Pop sent me for some advice. Things may not be working out so well with this marriage of his."

"Not the first time I've heard that," says the priest. "These proxy marriages – they never know what they're getting into. Come on in."

He ushers Marcello into the foyer where, under a stylized Christ on a bloodless cross, the two have a short discussion about church law. Marcello leaves ten minutes later feeling he can think clearly for the first time in a week.

"I want to sleep with you," he tells Ida in the Chevy that night.

She laughs. "You sleep with me all the time."

"No. I mean, really sleep with you and wake up in the morning together. In a bed. Like man and wife."

Ida looks at him seriously. "Okay, come to my room tonight."

"I have a better idea."

As usual, Marcello drives the Chevy out onto the concession roads, but bypasses the farm lanes where they usually park. A half hour passes without conversation, only the crackling of the car radio for company, until they see the mist from the Falls glistening under streetlights.

Marcello slows to a crawl as they pass the gorge. Tourists in orange plastic ponchos throng at the brink, balancing children on the stonework barrier. Colours burst into view, green, pink, blue, purple, shimmering over a vast emptiness.

Ida sticks her face out of the window: "*Allora!* The water has colour?"

"Only in summer. They shine lights from a tower."

Ida struggles to see the water behind the rainbow. "Why do they paint colours on Niagara Falls? Aren't they already a wonder of the world?"

"They just want to make it more interesting, I guess. When you see it all the time, the excitement kind of wears off." After a pause he adds: "We'll come back for a better look after we're married."

Ida stares at him. "*Che?*"

"We can get the church to annul your marriage," he answers, one hand on the steering wheel, the other holding Ida's hand. "All we have to do is get Pop to sign a paper saying it was never consummated. That means, you never slept together."

Ida shakes her head: "This, I'm sure he will not do."

"We'll see," says Marcello.

Within a few minutes, they have passed through the crush of cars near the Falls and find themselves alone, driving in darkness as they head upriver where farm fields and towns cling uncertainly to the shore. As roads peter into lanes, then dirt tracks, they bump along through scrub patches of birch; beyond them Ida can make out a squat building barely visible in the moonlight. Marcello kills the engine and the two sit for a moment listening to the call and response of the waves and the creaking of cicadas.

At the door Marcello searches in his jeans for a pocketknife, which he uses to *jimmy* the lock on the door (*what a strange word*, thinks Ida). The building smells of fish and sand and mould. Marcello doesn't want to turn on the lights. As Ida stands in the doorway, waiting for him to find a flashlight, she hears a flurry of panicked wings in the rafters.

"*Ucelli*?" she asks.

"Not birds. Bats. *Come se dice – pipistrelli.*"

She screams and throws her arms over her head. Laughing he pulls her to him. "Don't worry, that's an old wives' tale about bats getting caught in your hair."

"Old wives?"

"Just a dumb saying. English is full of them."

With Marcello leading the way, they find their way through a patch of scrubby trees out to the beach, a narrow stretch of hard-packed sand littered with pebbles and seaweed and the odd dead fish. The two of them stand looking at the crescent Moon dangling over the lake like a fishing lure, Marcello's arms wrapped around Ida from behind. "The Americans will be there soon. Imagine being the first one to touch the Moon."

"Very exciting," she agrees.

They stand in silence for a few moments looking up at the stars. Marcello has the feeling that they are actually the bright little eyes of animals, watching the two of them. They strip naked and swim just offshore, the lake as warm as bathwater. Marcello kisses and teases Ida, diving between her legs like a dolphin, Ida *shooshing* him: *Stop it, someone hears us Cello*, just before he pulls her giggling below the surface. They make love in the tug and release of the surf, Marcello's back grinding against hard sand and shells while Ida lowers herself onto him, hands braced against his shoulders.

Back in the cottage, Marcello chips a package of hot dogs out of the icebox with a fish knife and boils them on top of the stove in a pot so dented it barely sits upright on the burner. While they eat, Ida takes a folded paper out of her purse and spreads it on the table: a road map of Canada, much handled. Marcello points out places he's always wanted to visit: Montreal, Winnipeg, the Yukon. Ida shakes her head and runs her finger firmly along the west coast: "Horses and mountains and ranches and ocean."

"I guess you could learn how to ride," comments Marcello.

Ida yawns and stretches. "Oh, I know already to ride. My father, he teach me."

Marcello clears his throat. "Your father died in the War. Before you were born. Remember?"

Ida takes another bite of hot dog, chews it slowly and swallows before answering: "My second father, I speak about. After my mamma remarries."

Marcello opens his mouth, then shuts it. Best to let it go. For now.

Later, they lie side by side on a mattress softened by a threadbare beach towel, touching one another until they fall sleep. Marcello dreams that a rock is resting on his chest, speaking in a strange tongue. When he awakens in darkness, he reaches down and discovers that the rock is Ida's head. She's talking in her sleep in a language Marcello doesn't understand. Her dream-language is neither English nor Italian, nor French, which Marcello learned in school, nor Ukrainian or Polish, which he hears a lot in the neighbourhood, nor Portuguese or Greek, which some new *giusta-comes* speak. No, Ida's dream language is as jagged and hard-edged as broken glass, an entirely unfamiliar tongue. He props himself up on one arm and looks down at her.

"Are you from Mars, Ida?" he whispers, stroking her face as she mumbles mysterious words.

Ida gropes with her hand to see where Marcello is. He catches her fingers and kisses them.

"*Shhhh*, go back to sleep," he whispers.

When light floods the room through uncurtained windows, Marcello opens his eyes to a framed photograph of one of the Andolini uncles proudly holding up a fish on a line. A bedside table holds a stack of paperbacks, the pages bloated by water, perhaps left out in the rain or dropped in the lake; he reads the titles running down the cracked and faded spines:

*Airport.*
*Couples.*

*2001: A Space Odyssey.*
*Diamonds Are Forever.*

Ida is still asleep. He checks his watch: it's seven in the morning. Senior will get up soon and discover that the Chevy isn't in its usual spot and that Ida's bed hasn't been slept in. Blind as Senior might have been to their love affair up until now, he'll start to understand the way things are. They've spent the night together which means that Marcello has ruined Ida – not only taken her virginity, but soiled her reputation as a traditional Italian girl, which was the point of Senior taking her a proxy bride in the first place. Marcello believes that in Senior's eyes, Ida's worth will fall to less than nothing.

That'll make it easier when Marcello makes him sign whatever paper they need for an annulment – *an affidavit*, Father Ray called it. It's the only way to take Ida away from Senior honourably and make an honest woman of her without having to run and hide and pretend forever. Marcello is strong, he could dig ditches for a living. If he isn't to be a priest, he at least wants to live a peaceful, normal, decent life, properly married to Ida. Hell, maybe he'll even get the organist to play Pachelbel at the wedding.

## 9

*July 14*

"THIS IS HOW YOU honour your father, you bastard?" shouts Senior hoarsely.

Jagged bits of glass rain down on Marcello, splinters clinging to his hair, his jeans, even his eyelashes and the skin of this arms. He's lying on the floor, trying to avoid Senior's wild swings with the baseball bat. He's just smashed the cut glass vase holding the dozen red roses but he was aiming for Marcello's head.

Marcello tells himself that he should have anticipated Senior's rage. He's just grateful that when they got back, he told Ida to go upstairs and start packing; he said that once he'd thrashed things out with Senior, he'd take her to the Andolinis for safekeeping until the annulment came through. He hopes she doesn't come downstairs in response to all the ruckus.

At first it looked like the heart-to-heart with Senior was going to be, if not exactly civil, no worse than awkward. When they got back that morning, Marcello found him at the counter, looking confused; the first words out of his mouth were: "Junior, what you doing buying roses and candy for Ida?"

Marcello blinked. "She said they came from you."

"Like hell. You know how much these things cost?" Senior opened the Pot of Gold box and tossed a handful of chocolates into his mouth. "She no make breakfast today."

Marcello pulled himself up to his full height – a few inches taller than Senior – and said: "That's 'cause she was with me."

"What you talking about? Nothing open this early."

Marcello took a deep breath and launched into his speech. He started with the love-at-first-sight attraction between him and Ida, moving on to Senior's lies to get her over here. Then there was the fact that Ida was much closer to Marcello's age than to Senior's – *she's young enough to be your daughter, Pop.*

Encouraged by Senior's lack of response, he proceeded to their first kiss, followed by Ida's deflowering. Marcello thought he should leave that part in to make it clear to Senior that Ida was pure, up until four days ago, to give his father a sense of the depth of the attraction: they were helpless in the face of it, he explained. Senior stood through the entire speech with his mouth hanging open.

Then he went behind the counter and found the baseball bat.

Panting, unable to catch Marcello and connect the bat with his head, Senior starts hurling words: "You kill my first wife, when you give her the polio. Now you turn my second wife into a whore. Goddamn you to hell. Goddamn you to fucking hell. I spit on you, I curse you. You're not my son." Marcello thinks Senior is disowning him until he adds: "When your mother show up with you, I didn't even want you. *Why you not tell me you got a kid,* I say. *The marriage broker tell me to surprise you,* she say. I should of sent you back where you come from."

Marcello doesn't understand what he's hearing until the words *marriage broker* sink in. His mother Sofia must have been a proxy bride, like Ida.

"You're not my father?"

"You think I'd give my own blood away to the Andolinis?" rages Senior, and smashes the bat down on the pop cooler as Marcello jumps out of the way. Trapped in the corner next to the magazine rack, he takes Senior's next swing in the gut: winded but not wounded, he staggers toward the screen door, telling himself that Senior won't keep coming at him once they're out on the street. Again, he's misjudged Senior's rage: with Marcello backing up onto the stoop, Senior winds up and swings the bat hard into his ribs, sending him over the railing onto the sidewalk. His head hits the pavement like an exploding firecracker.

Pain crushes Marcello like a thousand football tackles, a million hits into the boards. Twin waves of nausea and agony rush up, pulling him into a sea filled with crucifixes and roses and chocolate boxes and Canadian Tire money; he feels like he's floating, watching the beating happen to some other guy on a distant shoreline.

Far, far away, he can hear shrill shouts. At first Marcello thinks the voice is Ida's and tries to gasp out *Run*. But when he sees a dirty face and dark eyes looking down at him, he realizes it's Bum Bum shouting *stop stop stop stop*, grabbing at Marcello's hands, trying to pull him to his feet. No hope.

The sky spinning over him, he sees Senior lift the bat into the clouds: instinctively, Marcello puts up his arms to protect his head, but the blow doesn't fall. Senior is tugging at something behind him: Christie Hryhorchuck, grabbing at the bat. *Stop it he'll hurt you*, Marcello tries to warn her, but the words won't come out. He still doesn't see Ida anywhere, thank God.

Senior swears at Christie, then disappears from sight as if he's been swept off his feet. All Marcello can see is blue sky, until the buttercup blonde head of Niagara Glen Kowalchuck looms into view, Bum Bum's tear-stained face close beside him.

Through the buzzing in his ears, he hears Kowalchuck's amazed voice say, "What the fucking hell is going on? Get him upstairs."

Somehow, someone (Kowalchuk? Bum Bum? Both?) pulls Marcello to his feet, where he teeters uncertainly, the world a merry-go-round. Canal Road looks like a dreamy panoramic 3D postcard: Senior is being held in a one-armed headlock by Stinky, blue tattoos bulging on his forearm; Christie holds the baseball bat on her shoulder as if heading to a game; Mrs. Hryhorchuck has come out on the stoop in her bathing suit, cleaning rag to her mouth. The shock on Mrs. H's face tells Marcello everything he needs to know about how he looks right now.

Propped between a tall body and a short one, he's being half-dragged, half-carried toward the front door of Kowalchuck Flowers until he vomits on his sneakers and falls into a void.

## 10

MARCELLO COMES-TO IN a slope-ceilinged room the bright yellow of a child's crayon sun. A man with the face of an unshaven bullfrog is looking down at him, the tell-tale scent of Sen-Sen barely masking the stale Hiram Walker on his breath. *Same brand as Pop*, he thinks: no, no, Senior's not his father, he's just found out his father is a question mark.

A bright light shines in his eyes. *Penlight*, Marcello registers. The bullfrog is holding it up as he peers at him. He can hear the man's breath wheeze.

"Don't worry, you're still a pretty boy. Thank your Pop for not smashing in your nose." Somewhere in the room, someone laughs. This must have been a joke.

The bullfrog man looks familiar. Marcello's brain gropes in the dark, trying to remember him. *Oh yeah, one of the craps players.* Sighing, he closes his eyes.

"Hey hey hey none of that," says the bullfrog man, shaking Marcello's hip. "Gotta stay awake."

"How you know it's a concussion?" says a voice.

"Lookit his eyes. I've seen it a million times with fighters. Got a couple of cracked ribs too. Nothing you can do but let 'em heal. Want me to tape him?"

"Go ahead," says the voice.

The bullfrog man gently slides an arm behind Marcello and moves him up to sitting. The pain is fierce, a sword running through one side of his chest and out the other.

"Ida?" he moans.

"Not even close, sweetheart," grunts the bullfrog.

"How long before he can walk normal?" asks the voice.

"Day or two. But like I said, you gotta keep him awake for a day and a night to make sure you don't die in his sleep."

The voice says: "Guess I better get him a nursemaid."

After the bullfrog leaves, Marcello's brain skips over time like a stone on a pond. At first, he's still in the bright yellow room, on a narrow bed, a plaid comforter tossed over him despite the heat. When he pivots his head, he can see that the walls are covered with athletic ribbons and awards; one large framed black and white photograph is of a white-haired teenager in a football uniform, a plaque screwed into it reading *Zenon 'Glen' Kowalchuck, Captain, St. Dismas Bandits, City Champions 1955.* Except for the low rumble of a television from somewhere, the room is very quiet. Despite the bullfrog's warnings, Marcello dozes.

He wakes up to a sensation of movement. Someone is shaking his legs, trying to rouse him. Opening his eyes, he sees Bum Bum. The kid pulls a pack of Export As from his pants and taps out a cigarette, holding it toward Marcello as if offering medicine. When Marcello drops the cigarette, Bum Bum puts the smoke between his swollen lips and lights him up.

Marcello relaxes a little as the smoke fill his lungs. It's better than nothing: he vaguely remembers the bullfrog saying to the voice *And nothing for the pain neither for twenty-four hours, after that he can pop 222s.*

"Where's Ida?" he mumbles.

"Andolinis'. Kowalchuck afraid your Pop gonna kill her."

Marcello says a silent prayer of thanks as Bum Bum gets up and leans over him, tear tracks still visible through the dirt on his face. "C'mon, I help you get up. Something on TV you gonna wanna watch."

In the main room of the flat, Marcello lies with his head on a velvet souvenir cushion from the Ripley's Believe It or Not Museum, the skin of his back sweaty against a plastic couch cover. Old Mrs. K. is spread out in a recliner next to him, feet up, eyes on the TV. Bum Bum is fixing them tumblers of Tang and bowls of Cheerios brimming with milk.

A TV voice is saying: *All report they are 'go' for the mission... the swing arm will now come back to its fully retracted position... Launch Director Rocco Petrone now gives a 'go'.*

On television, white smoke pours from the Saturn rocket as it thrusts skyward: *Lift off! Tower cleared! We have lift off at thirty-two minutes past the hour, the lift off of Apollo 11. We're through the region of maximum dynamic pressure now. This is Houston, you are good for staging.* Then they hear the voice of Neil Armstrong – through the static he sounds strong, confident, almost joyous: *Hey Houston, Apollo 11. This Saturn gave us a magnificent ride. It was beautiful.*

Marcello, Bum Bum and Mrs. K. stare at the screen as the camera follows the rocket turning from a flying white skyscraper into a distant gleam in the blue. Mrs. K. mumbles something in Ukrainian that sounds like a prayer. Marcello makes the sign of the cross. Bum Bum spoons up Cheerios, burps and asks, "You think they find green girls up there, like on *Star Trek*?"

Marcello laughs, then winces at the pain. "No, just rocks and craters."

"Why bother go?" wonders Bum Bum.

Later, with Walter Cronkite interviewing everyone from the head of Mission Control to the guy selling hot dogs at Cape Kennedy, Bum Bum pulls a book out of his pants: Marcello's beaten copy of *I, Robot*.

"I can't make the story go on my own."

Marcello opens the book but the words stagger all over the page. "My head hurts too much to read, Pasquale."

The boy nudges him. "You gotta stay awake."

Marcello stares at the book until he finally focuses his eyes, then starts reading. Mrs. K. turns to listen.

In the middle of the chapter, a thought occurs to Marcello: stopping, he looks at Bum Bum and asks: "Was it you brought the flowers and chocolates to Ida?"

The boy shakes his head, then nods. "I bring them over, but they not from me. Wedding present from Kowalchuck."

Marcello considers this – *why did Ida say they were from Senior?* – until his train of thought slides to the floor along with the book. When Bum Bum puts it back in his hands, he starts reading one word after another again but can't keep the thread of the story in his head. Bum Bum sighs in contentment and leans against him, the pressure of his body painful yet comforting against Marcello's taped ribs.

Some time that day – morning, afternoon, who knows – with Marcello still dizzy and chain-smoking Export As, Kowalchuck shows up at the flat. Pulling one of the captain's chairs out from the poker table, he sits in front of Marcello, elbows on knees. The dial on his watch reads quarter to three. Marcello has to work hard to figure out how many hours he's been there.

"I can't believe I'm saying this, but I've come to make the peace," Kowalchuck tells him.

Marcello coughs painfully. "Ida okay?"

Kowalchuck chuckles, patting Marcello's leg. "One track mind. Your father sure as hell don't want his bride no more, now that you ruined her. She's safe and sound with Prima. The Chevy too. But I'm owed a shitload of money for bringing her over."

"I'll look after it. Ida's with me now," says Marcello firmly, then asks: "How much?"

"Two thousand."

Marcello gives a low groan.

"That job I told you about. You do it, we call it even. I'll even take your gambling debts into consideration. It goes about four days from now – you oughta be okay by then."

"I won't beat anyone up," says Marcello.

Kowalchuck waves a hand dismissively. "I don't need nothing like that. Just a big, smart guy who makes an impression. You talk good. You can help me bring pressure to bear."

"What if I don't?" asks Marcello. As usual, he wants all the facts.

"Then I keep the woman myself," says Kowalchuck. "I could use someone to look after Ma. Cook, clean. Other shit, too."

Marcello takes a moment to weigh the odds. On one side, Ida. On the other, Kowalchuck's job. The decision is clear. He offers Kowalchuck his hand.

"Now heal up so you can settle your debt," says Kowalchuck. "Then you can run off and live happy ever after, like fucking Blondie and Dagwood."

## 11

*July 19*

"His job was to scare the woman. Yours was to scare the kid. Wasn't that obvious?" asks Kowalchuck, as he walks Marcello to the car.

"Nothing was obvious," says Marcello, fighting a desire to vomit.

He notices the wet grass under his boots, the phlegmy catch in Kowalchuck's throat, the frantic barking of a dog in the distance. Every sound is so crisp, every detail so sharply defined, that they press themselves deeply into his mind, returning to him years later in nightmares and illness.

The stars shine down on Marcello and Kowalchuck, a thousand thousand eyes witnessing their actions.

*It wasn't supposed to be like this*, thinks Marcello.

All he was supposed to do was stand there and give some fat businessman something to think about. *You might have to say a few firm words*, Kowalchuck assured him. That's all it should take to inspire fear, persuading the guy to do whatever it is that Kowalchuck wants him to do. A good thing, since all that's holding Marcello together are the bandages around his ribs and a handful of 222s.

Pain enhances, rather than detracts, from the impression he wants to create. With his black clothing and boots and his physical size, Marcello easily inspires fear. His swollen and bruised face only heightens the sense of him being a dangerous man.

*Look at this guy – somebody turned him into mincemeat and he's still ready for a fight. Want to take a poke at him? Be my guest.*

It's a bluff, like in poker. Marcello's only consolation is that he's too deeply wounded to hurt anyone else.

Kowalchuck has already outlined the rules for this job:

They all arrive together in one car: Kowalchuck, Marcello, and a third man of Kowalchuck's choosing. After, the Chevy will be waiting on a concession road so Marcello can make a clean getaway.

Kowalchuck does all the talking. Unless he asks you a direct question, you keep your mouth shut. If anyone else asks you a question, you don't answer.

Don't do anything unless Kowalchuck tells you to.

Wear black: a close-fitting, short-sleeved black tee shirt, black pants, black combat boots. You want them to see how strong you are. How you could crush them with one hand. It's part of the intimidation thing. Make sure the cracked ribs are taped up nice and tight so you don't slouch.

No improvising.

When Bum Bum helps him walks downstairs from Mrs. K's flat to the Impala, Kowalchuck is at the wheel, the other man in back. Kowalchuck waves Marcello into the shotgun seat. Glancing back, he sees that the other man is the broken-down biker from Hamilton. Stan.

"Open the glove, Junior. Something in there for you," says Kowalchuck.

Marcello opens it to find a set of brass knuckles. "What do I need these things for?"

"Makes things go smoother."

Marcello's chest is aching badly now; the cracked ribs are dulled by painkillers but nothing touches the burning on his chest. The scratches have started bleeding again, a sign that he's about to make a mistake, as if the brass knuckles and Stan's presence weren't enough to tell him that. He knows he should leave right now, but he can't get out of a moving car; there's a sense of irrevocability to the whole thing that makes him feel lightheaded. Otherworldly.

They drive through darkness for about thirty minutes, maybe forty. Still not thinking straight, Marcello forgets to time the trip. Later, when he attempts to recreate the route, to figure out exactly which farm lane they pulled into, he won't be able to.

From the farm lane, they pull onto a long gravel driveway cutting through the frontage of a tender fruit farm: Marcello can make out the expanse of strawberry fields and beyond it, a peach orchard. On farms like this, there is usually a dog or two, mean as hell. The kind that would go for the wheels of your car even before you got out. Not tonight.

They park in the yard of a weathered grey farmhouse, the tall saltbox shape of every other farmhouse Marcello has ever seen, and walk to the front door. It's a strangely suburban door, with a painted glass window of geese rising off a lake, out of place against the peeling clapboard walls.

Stan walks along the outside wall of the house. Marcello can hear the snips of wire cutters in the darkness as he severs the Bell line, isolating everyone inside the house from the civilized world beyond.

"Take off your jacket, Marcello," says Kowalchuck, quietly, as they stand at the door. "You have to let them *see* you." Marcello pulls off the jacket and slings it over one arm, the brass knuckles weighing down one pocket.

Kowalchuck doesn't knock. He pushes open the door and stands in the hallway with Stan on his left and Marcello on his right.

They can hear the sound of a radio. It isn't music or anything you'd hear on a regular station, but a monotonous voice reciting weather observations:

*Township of Bramborough. Ten-oh-five p.m. Winds five miles per hour out of the south-south-west. Temperature, sixty-eight. Probability of precipitation ten percent.*

A woman walks into the hallway. She's thin, washed out, with a faded blonde dye job, her hair pulled tightly back off a face that has seen too much sun and wind; she looks skinned, like the carcass of a squirrel. Her eyelashes and eyebrows are so pale, she reminds Marcello of a battered angel, in an apron and rubber gloves dripping with dish soap.

"You again," she says to Kowalchuck. Her voice sounds creaky and hoarse, as if she has a sore throat.

"We have to talk to George," Kowalchuck tells her neutrally. He might as well be the meter reader.

A man comes to the door, a sunburned guy in overalls, broken-down leather slippers and a faded tee shirt reading *Round-Up*. This is the fat businessman Kowalchuck told him about?

"What the hell are you doing here? I've already given you my answer!" He's almost snarling, but Marcello can tell he's scared; he keeps stepping forward, then retreating.

"Wrong answer," says Kowalchuck, very calmly. "Just to remind you, George, you're still into me for ten thousand. Saying no doesn't make any sense. Wouldn't want your family hurt."

"I've been paying you when I can, for Chrissake. I'm going to call the cops."

"Go ahead," says Kowalchuck. "I'll be happy to tell them what you've got planted in the field."

The farmer hesitates; Marcello realizes now why he's so scared. He's stuck. Made some bad choices that are catching up with him. Like Marcello. Probably like Ida, too.

"Who's this guy?" asks the farmer, gesturing at Marcello.

Kowalchuck glances down at Marcello's bare hands, folded in front of him; the brass knuckles are still in his pocket. "This is my son. Mean son of a bitch, meaner than me. I brought him along to spend some time with your son, to help persuade you."

That's when the boy comes into the hallway. He can't be more than thirteen, with a wide, reddish face and a shaggy thatch of blonde hair. He looks like his mother. He's wearing a Minnesota North Stars hockey jersey that the mother probably found in some thrift store. No kid wears a jersey from a lame-ass expansion team unless they have no choice. When Marcello sees the boy, he realizes finally and absolutely what a mistake he's made. But there's no turning back now.

The mother grabs the boy by his arm and stutters, "Ethan, go back, go back now, in, into the kitchen and finish your work."

But the boy shakes off her hand and stands looking from one to the other of them. He's short for his age, hasn't had his growth spurt yet, his face still delicate, hairless and thin, almost pretty.

Marcello stares at Ethan and thinks *There wasn't supposed to be a kid*, but of course it never came up, one way or the other. The boy looks at Marcello and takes a quick step back. Marcello notices a spreading stain on the boy's blue jeans and the smell of urine.

He's just scared a thirteen-year-old into peeing his pants.

Marcello is filled with a powerful sense of self-disgust. And he hasn't even left the front door yet.

Marcello, Stan, Ethan and his mother are in the kitchen. Marcello can hear the farmer's voice, shouting in another room, but he can't hear Kowalchuck's replies; of course not, because he stays in control. The man doesn't know what's going on in the other room with his family. He can only imagine what Marcello and Stan are doing to them. Marcello wonders what Kowalchuck is telling him.

The kid is sitting at the table in front of a textbook. *Summer school*, thinks Marcello. He recognizes the book, which he almost knows off by heart: *Pathways to Algebra: 2nd Edition*. He glances down involuntarily to check the kid's answers. Then he realizes how ridiculous this is and averts his eyes. Bad guys don't correct their victim's homework.

He knows he can't reassure these people or comfort them in any way. They think he's the one Clint Eastwood comes in and shoots. There's no point in smiling or offering false niceties: he came here tonight to scare them and he's doing a hell of a job.

"This will be over soon," says Marcello reassuringly. "No one is going to get hurt."

"We're already hurt," rasps the woman.

Dressed in the same tight black fatigues as Marcello, Stan has been sitting quietly on the other side of the room, on a stool pulled up under a bulletin board with notices tacked to it: *Egg Pick-Up, Sunday. St. Dunstan's Fair, Aug. 12.* A recipe for *Easy No-bake Quiche*, clipped out of the Hamilton *Spectator*. A blue ribbon from the Niagara District Fair reading *Best in Show, Peach Preserves.*

"What's through that door, there?" asks Stan.

The woman looks where he's pointing. "The hallway."

"Show me," commands Stan.

*What's he doing?* wonders Marcello.

The woman stands up cautiously and goes to the door. "The hallway leads to the living room. There," she points out.

"And where's that stairway go?"

"Upstairs bedrooms," says the woman, almost in a whisper. She's losing her voice.

"Show me," repeats Stan. She hesitates. He walks up behind her and gives a little push to the small of her back, making her stumble forward.

"Mum!" says the kid, standing up. He glances at Marcello, who has no idea what to do.

"Sit down," he finally says to Ethan, who does.

He can hear Stan and the woman walking up the stairs.

"What's that guy doing with my mother?" asks Ethan, his voice cracking. Marcello can see the tremors of fear in the boy's body; he's shaking as though he's in a cold wind.

*If the guy asks you a question, don't answer.*

"Take it easy," says Marcello, breaking the code of silence again.

"Don't let him hurt her," begs the boy. "Those guys've been here before. They're nuts."

*What makes you think I won't hurt her? Or hurt you?* wonders Marcello.

"I won't let anything happen to her," Marcello says, unsure of how to make good on this promise. "Look, I'll go upstairs and check on things. You stay here."

He has to leave Ethan alone in the kitchen; if he has any sense, the kid will arm himself while Marcello is out of the room, there's a big butcher's cleaver, right there in a block on the counter. Marcello considers taking the cleaver upstairs with him, so that Ethan doesn't attack him when he returns, but what's the point: there must be lots of potential weapons in this kitchen and he can't gather them all. He's sure the kid won't leave this house without his mother. Anyway, the closest farm is a good five miles away. And if he tries to help his father, he'll come face to face with Kowalchuck.

On the second floor, Marcello is met by a line of closed doors, and one open one. It's the master bedroom. When he enters, he sees Stan with his pants down, thrusting forward toward the bed, where he's pinned the woman between his legs; Marcello can't see her face, but he can hear her gagging.

"Kowalchuck says for you to go out and start the car," says Marcello in the calmest, most forceful voice he can muster. "George signed. We can leave."

"In a minute," answers Stan.

"Right NOW, Stan, right fucking NOW," says Marcello in the tone he employs when he catches kids trying to shoplift in the store. "I heard sirens. Want to wait around, find out who they're for?"

Stan turns to glare at Marcello, then steps away from the bed and tugs up his pants. The woman is left sprawled on the bed, a puddle of pale skin and blonde hair, her face mottled; she starts coughing.

As he leaves the room, he says to Marcello, "Be my guest."

Marcello stands listening to the sound of Stan going down the stairs, through the hallway, out the front door. The woman is crying and spitting into a tissue from the bedside table. He wants to comfort her, but he's pretty sure he's just going to scare her, if he touches her.

"I'm going to take you back downstairs to Ethan," Marcello says. "Do you want to wash your face?"

She nods and heads out of the room and down the hall, not looking at Marcello. Inside the bathroom, she coughs and runs water, then the toilet flushes; she's making herself throw up, Marcello suspects. When she comes out, looking damp and exhausted, her lips chafed and raw, Marcello takes her arm but she wrenches it away from him.

"You're animals," she tells Marcello fiercely. "I don't consider you human. I just want you to know that."

"Okay," says Marcello. "But I'm trying to help you."

"Oh, I see, *help* me" she rasps. "If you want to *help*, shoot your friends."

*No gun,* thinks Marcello. *None of us is armed. The only weapon we have is me.*

When they reach the kitchen, Marcello sees that Ethan hasn't left the spot where he left him. The butcher's cleaver is still in the block.

*Why didn't you try to arm yourself? I gave you your best chance,* thinks Marcello in frustration.

Over the panicked up-down of the farmer's voice in the next room, he can hear the engine of the Impala idling in the yard. Stan must have believed them. He sticks his hand in his pocket and brushes his fingers against the brass knuckles. He could take both Kowalchuck and Stan with them, maybe, then drive off in the Impala with the kid and his mother. He could rescue them, bring them somewhere safe, and then, with a clear conscience, go to the Andolinis, collect Ida and disappear. He's still imagining this when the kitchen door swings open and Kowalchuck walks in. He grabs the woman by the arm.

"Time to let George have a look at his family." He glances around the kitchen. "Where's Stan?"

Marcello, feeling a wave of dizziness, steadies himself against the counter. "In the car."

"What the fuck for? We're not finished here." He looks at Ethan, sitting at the table. "You ain't done nothing to the kid."

"I was just supposed to scare him, you said," says Marcello uneasily.

Kowalchuck glares at Marcello, seething with impatience. Still gripping the woman, he backhands Ethan across the face, knocking him off his chair. The woman screams and twists away, dropping to the floor with her son. Ethan is crying, his nose gushing blood. Marcello's hand tightens around the brass knuckles in his pocket – he's got to end this now – when a shout comes from the other room. It's George's voice: "For Christ's sake, stop it, I'll sign!"

They walk out to the Impala, side by side.

"You have to scare the families," explains Kowalchuck. "Women and kids bring pressure to bear. So you have to put *them* under pressure."

"That was more than pressure. Stan hurt her."

"Depends what you mean by 'hurt'," says Kowalchuck, shrugging.

Marcello feels a wave of nausea.

Marcello sits in the back seat of the Impala as they drive him to his car.

"Except for Junior screwing around, a good night," says Kowalchuck from behind the wheel. "We scared that guy shitless."

"Got what you wanted?" asks Stan.

Kowalchuck nods. "Signed right on the dotted line. The developer's ready to plough under the peach orchard tomorrow. That's where they're gonna put the man-made lake."

Stan laughs. "You're shittin' me. Lake Ontario's right there."

"Full of dead fish," points out Kowalchuck. "Man-made lake's nice, like a swimming pool. It's going to be a big selling feature once houses go in. People'll pay through the nose for that kind of shit." He sighs in contentment. "I can finally get Ma into a good old folks' home, instead of one of those barns where they leave everyone sitting in their own crap."

Kowalchuck stops the car on the concession road and waves Marcello out of the back seat. Through the window, he hands him a thick envelope.

"What's this?"

"Two hunnert. Take it. That farm's worth a hunnert times more'n the candy store and Ida and your gambling debt put together. Land development, that's the future, Junior. Everybody wants a little place out in the country. Even though you screwed up, you should have a taste."

"Keep it," says Marcello trying to shove back the envelope.

Kowalchuck waves him off. "Give it to the missions."

Marcello looks around him in the darkness. "Where's the Chevy?"

Kowalchuck points down the road. "'Bout ten miles west of here, parked on Concession Eleven."

Marcello leans down to grip the edge of the window. "Are you kidding? It'll take me all night to walk that far. You said you'd bring me there."

"Change of plan. We got stuff to do." With that, Kowalchuck hits the gas. The Impala accelerates down the road until it's swallowed in darkness. Marcello bends over and vomits in the ditch. Then he starts walking.

As he learned in grade nine science class: *Everything in life is physics!*

Every action is matched by an equal and opposite reaction. Marcello liked watching science teachers demonstrate this with a set of swinging metal balls suspended from rods; you set the first ball in motion, which hits the one beside it, which sets that one swinging, and within seconds, they're all swinging.

Transference of energy.

The thug threatens. The innocents suffer. Not just tonight, not just here, but forever and everywhere.

As he stumbles along the edge of the concession road in darkness, he starts to imagine that boy, Ethan, showing up at the candy store. What would Marcello say to him?

*Ethan! Good to see you! How's your Mom?*

*She'd be a lot happier if all you guys were dead.*

He has to make an Act of Contrition. That woman will never be the same again, or the boy. He has to atone. But what's he going to do? He can't give them their farm back or erase their memories of tonight.

Dawn brings out the farm trucks, heading into town to collect that day's fruit pickers. Limping along the shoulder of the road in a daze, Marcello almost forgets to stick out his thumb. A farmer finally stops to offer him a lift in the back of his pickup. Marcello checks his watch, waiting for his vision to blend the two sets of hands into one. He's been walking about five hours.

Marcello rests against the wall of the truck bed and turns his face into the wind, the morning coolness soothing him, and says a prayer of thanks. He watches the sun come up over Lake Ontario, grapefruit-pink streaked with gold. Pretty as hell. Somewhere on the road ahead is his getaway car. All he needs to do now is to drive to the Andolinis, get Ida, and leave. Then he can spend the rest of his life being a good man to atone for what he's just done.

Marcello is both surprised and relieved when he finally catches sight of the back of his car, parked on the verge of the concession road, just like Kowalchuck said. He waves his thanks into the rear-view of the truck and the farmer nods back, pulling over onto the shoulder. Finding the car unlocked, Marcello lifts a hand again to indicate to the farmer that he's fine now, and the truck drives away, raising a cloud of gravel dust.

It's only when Marcello climbs behind the steering wheel that he remembers that he doesn't have the ignition key. He checks in the glove and under the driver's seat. No key. *Jesus.*

Putting his head down on the steering wheel, he allows himself to close his eyes for a minute. When he awakes, stiff-necked, the angle of the sun through the windshield tells him he's been asleep for some time. He checks his watch: it's eleven o'clock in the morning. At least he feels a little rested. But the pain in his ribs has returned full-force, the painkillers having worn off.

He shakes out a handful of 222s and chews them dry. The chalky taste makes him thirsty. The water in the irrigation ditch beside the car is probably full of chemicals from Hooker and DuPont, but what the hell does he care? Getting out, he crouches to scoop a handful of tepid water into his mouth: it tastes like bitter soap.

Back behind the steering wheel, he takes a few minutes to let the pills kick in and tries to think through this new problem. He's still got his tools in the glove from repairing the stove: screwdriver, wire-cutters, electrical tape.

He wraps his fingertips in the tape and uses the screwdriver to pop out the ignition. From under the dash, he tugs out three live wires – one red, one blue, one green – and touches them together. The engine grinds, the ignition sends out a shower of sparks and, despite the electrical tape, the tips of Marcello's fingers sizzle, but in seconds, the starter catches and the engine turns over. Marcello twists the three wires together and braces himself. The car is moving. *Houston, we have lift off.*

It's a cloudless day, the air fresh. On the other side of the lake, he can make out the Toronto skyline, the muscular arm of the Gardiner Expressway, even the ominous black slabs of the new bank towers. Somewhere in that tangle of billboards and highrises is the mother house of the Passionist Order of St. John, where his name is written backwards in a book: *Travato, Marcello*, born in Piacenza, Italy, January 1950. By now, they have surely received the letter from Father Ray, recommending Marcello for early admission so that he can be rushed into a more saintly life.

He averts his eyes from the skyline. His calling to the priesthood is in ashes, crushed with the last cigarette he smoked from the package stuffed in his pocket. Ida is his calling now.

Along the lakeshore road, willow trees drip long fingers into muddy strawberry fields, grape rows roll to the blue horizon, peach trees twist their knotted shoulders toward the sun. Everything is warm and sweet and juicy, like Ida. Signs reading *Cherries Raspberries Plums Peaches Apricots* call out to him to touch and squeeze and bite before the earth goes back to sleep like a woman whose lover has left her bed.

He turns on the radio and gets the news: *NASA Mission Control reports it's all systems go for the landing of Apollo 11 scheduled for...*

Marcello changes stations, trolling the dial until he hears the Beach Boys. The Chevy's overtaxed engine grinds its way up the steep Niagara Escarpment to the *a cappella* lyrics of *Barbara Ann*. Radio blasting, Marcello bullets past no-nonsense cornfields and black blocky beef cattle that already look like Sunday roasts, raising the eyebrows of upright men on tractors.

At last, he pulls into the long driveway leading to a high red brick farmhouse surrounded by a cluster of modern bungalows, like a mother with a brood of children. The Andolini men will be out in the fields but he knows exactly where to find the women.

He parks the car beside the old farmhouse and heads out back to the summer kitchen. Through the screen door, he's met by a blast of steamy heat: Prima, Gina and some of the little girls are canning peaches, the table before them a sea of Certo bottles and glass jars brimming with sun-yellow fruit. On the stove, pots of water are at a furious boil. Wiping dripping hair from their faces with rubber-gloved hands, the Andolini women stare at him without recognition. Over the last few weeks, he's become unrecognizable as the Marcello they once knew.

Finally realizing who he is, Prima pulls off her rubber gloves and comes to him, her hands raised to his bruised face. "*Carino*, what happen to you?"

"You look like hell," clarifies Gina.

"Where's Ida?" asks Marcello.

The women trade glances.

"Gone," says Gina. "The one-armed man came yesterday and took her away."

*Stinky. What the hell is going on?*

Marcello allows himself to be a pushed into a chair, Prima already placing a cup of coffee and a *cornetto* in front of him. He tries to calm himself but his questions run in circles. Why did they let her go with Stinky? (*One-arm man say he taking Ida to you.*) Where did he say they were going? (*He say nothing.*) What was he driving? (*A Ford, maybe – or Chrysler – beh, all these cars today look the same, not like the old days.*) Did Ida seem upset?

"Hard to tell with that one," mutters Gina.

Prima caresses his face, making him feel like a little kid: "Marcello, listen to me: you have to forget that woman. She is your father's wife. She bewitch you. She make you forget the most important thing of all, your calling."

Marcello looks up at the crucifix over the kitchen counter: one hangs in every room of this house. "Nonna, I'm not sure I ever really had one."

Prima takes both his hands in hers: "You hurt. You all confuse! Stay with us. You don't have to go home to your father."

"He's not my father. Did you know?"

Prima closes her eyes, and nods.

"I'm not even really Marcello Trovato Junior, am I?"

Prima shakes her head. "Your father a stonemason who die under a wall when an earthquake come. Your mother's family, all dead in a bombing in the War. She marry Senior to look after you. Then, she die." He can feel Prima's hands trembling in his. "*Tragedia, tragedia.*"

"Who am I, then?" Marcello wants to know.

"Your name is *Michaele*, like the archangel. Your father's name, *non lo so.*"

With his hands gripped by his adoptive grandmother's, in the deeply comforting warmth of the summer kitchen where he spent so much of his childhood, the buzz of the peach tree cicadas filling the air outside, and the sugary breeze wafting through the door, Marcello pictures himself staying here forever.

He kisses Prima. Then, unclasping the gold chain from around his neck, he pours the tortured man into her hand.

## 12

*July 20, 1969*

MARCELLO DRIVES BACK TO Shipman's Corners in silence. No music, no news. He pretends that time has stopped and that his life will simply skip forward to a happy ending, that he'll cruise by a street corner and glimpse Ida in her white blouse and skirt, suitcase beside her, waving a handkerchief to signal him to stop. *Cello, I've been waiting for you!*

No such luck.

Pasquale, he thinks, will know where she is: he always seems to know everything. But for the first time in memory, he's nowhere to be found.

*Damn that kid anyway*, he thinks, cruising strangely quiet streets. He checks the foundry and slaughterhouse where the men turn their palms up and shake their heads. *Haven't seen him in a couple days.* But one worker knows the address of Pasquale's parents' house. Marcello scribbles it in a matchbook and drives to the ramshackle one-story.

An ancient woman in a black dress and headscarf sits in a lawn chair on the front stoop; too old to be Bum Bum's mother, Marcello can only assume she's his Nonna.

"*Dové Pasquale?*" he asks the old woman. She shrugs.

The front door is open; cautiously Marcello walks up the steps of the stoop and peers in. The old Nonna stares at him suspiciously but doesn't ask what he's doing.

He enters the house.

There's nothing in it. *Almost* nothing. A couple of broken-down kitchen chairs. A mattress on the floor of the front room. (The Nonna's?) A bucket. A plastic crucifix with a faded palm frond stuck behind it. A bank calendar dated January 1966 tacked to the wall.

*The home of a compulsive gambler*, thinks Marcello. One who loses and loses and keeps staking whatever he has around him so that he can lose again. He'll bet anything, including his kid.

There's no sign of Bum Bum or either of his parents. No wonder he sleeps out in the alleyways at night. Marcello leaves the house through the back door and gets back in the car. There's only one place left to try now: Canal Road.

The street, he's relieved to see, is deserted: in this heat, everyone would normally be out on their porches and front stoops drinking beer and yelling at their kids in the street. But with Apollo 11 hurtling toward the Moon, the neighbourhood is indoors watching Walter Cronkite interview the astronauts' wives.

He parks in the craps players' alley and walks across the street to Italian Tobacco & Sweets. A CLOSED sign is on the door, the lights are off and everything is locked up tight, even the storeroom window. But when he steps away from the store and looks up at the window of the flat, he's puzzled to see something white, flattened against the glass – a sheet maybe?

Standing in front of the store, Marcello's ear picks up a sound, a low, steady hum that seems to be coming from the building. He walks up to the exterior wall and places his hands against the weather-beaten grey clapboard: through his fingertips, he can feel a vibration, as if the building is trembling.

Marcello takes the stairs of the fire escape quickly, fishes for the key in his pants and unlocks the door. When it swings open, he finds himself looking at something so bright and hot it dazzles his eyes and warms his skin. Two giant lights blaze, the size of garbage can lids, a Panavision camera on a tripod standing on the table, its lens pointed down at the couch. Electrical cables crisscross the room like fat orange snakes, their heads all meeting in a splitter shoved into the room's only wall socket. They're sucking away at the power like a mass of leeches in a bog.

Someone has moved the TV up here. The sound is down but he can see a scratchy image of an astronaut (*Armstrong?*)

bouncing down a ladder from the lunar lander. *The first man on the Moon*, thinks Marcello in amazement, but the flat itself is even more surprising. The front room has been turned into a caricature of the Sea of Tranquility, cardboard flats painted the lurid orange-yellow of processed cheese, craters clumsily drawn with felt tip pens still scattered on the floor. A black sheet stickered with silver and gold stars provides an unconvincing backdrop of outer space. The air has a sweet vomity smell; someone has been sick in the corner amongst an army of empty peppermint schnapps bottles. That's when Marcello notices the girl asleep in a pile of pillows. It's one of the twins – Jane, he thinks – snoring, wearing only her white tasselled majorette boots. Her skin has been painted a bright, shiny green like a lily pad. Two silver antennae bob from her head.

Legs spread, Kowalchuck sprawls on the couch, naked except for his socks and a pair of briefs caught around one ankle, the other twin straddling his lap. Like her sister, Judy is white-booted, her bare, green-skinned back to Marcello.

"Junior! Join the celebration." Kowalchuck shouts when he sees Marcello, welcoming him like an old friend. "You missed the shoot! But you're just in the time for the whatsamcallit, after-party. Grab a twin and I'll turn on the camera."

"I'm here for Ida," says Marcello, glancing around; he's relieved not to see her here.

Kowalchuck puts his hand on the back of Judy's lolling head. "Blondie's mine now. Along with this shitty store. Had to evict your Pop, I'm afraid."

Marcello wants desperately to beat this man down to nothingness, rendering him into bone and gristle and blood, like a stain on the slaughterhouse floor. He puts his hand in his pocket and feels the brass knuckles.

As if reading his mind, Kowalchuck grins. "I know you haven't got the balls to kill me, Junior. You couldn't even bring yourself to slap a kid. Even if you did, a thousand other guys will show up to take my place. I'm immortal."

The twin in his embrace – Judy, Marcello thinks – rolls her head to peer at him over her shoulder. "Wanna party, Cello?" she slurs. Her hands are braced against Kowalchuck's knees, fingernails painted the same creamsicle shade as Claudia's.

"I'm taking you and your sister home," answers Marcello. As he stoops to gather Jane from the floor, Ida appears in the bedroom door. Swaying a little, she clasps a silver bikini top in her fist, between her silver breasts. Even her hair has been turned silver. When she sees Marcello, the top slips from her hand and her face collapses into silver tears.

"Marcello, run, he kill you," she whispers. "Go now, don't look at me."

Kowalchuck cranes his head backwards at them. "You done a good job breaking Ida in, Junior. Stan and Stinky and me, we hardly had to force her at all."

Ida shines like a mirror. The lights are like huge suns, making the paint on her face drip to the floor. Through the door behind her, he sees Stan, face down on the bed, pants to his knees, thrusting. Pasquale is barely visible beneath him. The boy's face is buried in the blue counterpane, his arms hanging limply over the sides of the bed.

*We've gone to hell*, realizes Marcello.

He now knows the source of that low malevolent hum shaking the building: it's the sound of electricity with no place to go, unfocused energy pulsing through the old knob and tube wiring, into the fat orange cables, round and round in a never-ending circuit. With no breaker to trip, the electricity is over-amping, urgently looking for some place to go to ground.

Marcello puts his hand in his pocket, closing them around the brass knuckles. He pulls them out slowly and shows them to Kowalchuck.

"You're right: I don't have the guts to kill you. Here, you take them."

When Kowalchuck rises from the couch, Judy slides off him like a blanket. He walks slowly toward Marcello, penis bobbing, empty eyes fixed on the brass knuckles. They are a weapon, after all.

*Electricity used to be considered a mysterious, unexplainable force, not unlike the Holy Spirit,* according to Marcello's grade twelve physics teacher, an elderly priest who invoked the names of Edison and Tesla in tones usually reserved for saints. He spoke of electricity as a gift, something natural and powerful that God had bestowed upon the earth. *Just look up when you see a lightning storm if you don't believe me,* he lectured. It was not, he cautioned, a power invented or harnessed by man, but God's gift that man accidentally discovered and learned how to tame. *Like a lion,* he said. *If you mistreat it, it can kill you.*

And this, it turns out, is true. When Marcello tosses the brass knuckles toward the exposed condenser coils at the top of the fridge, Kowalchuck grabs at them.

The electricity shows itself as a bright line, thin as wire, an arc connecting Kowalchuck to the brass knuckles to the fridge, in an unbroken circuit of metal and flesh. The electrical charge flashes around this tight circle. Kowalchuck's naked body takes on a whiplash shape as he spasms and a sulfurous smell rises as his skin scorches and his lungs, heart and brain start to cook inside him. Sparks shoot from the condenser coils before he collapses to the floor. Flames leap from the fridge coils, to the plaster walls, to the curtains, to the plywood floor. The glass in the windows starts to shimmer and run, reverting to its true liquid state.

The bedroom doorway blazing, Stan is the first one out, pants around his knees as he hurtles down the fire escape. Marcello yells to Ida to get moving as he goes through the burning doorway to pull Pasquale into his arms. The boy is limp and light as a sackful of sticks, but the weight of his body sets off a stabbing pain in Marcello's ribs. Groaning, he throws him over his shoulder in a fireman's carry and runs back into the main room, where he bundles a twin under each arm like a sack of sugar; they descend together, flames running down the stairway behind them. Marcello's cracked ribs cry out under his load of three children as Ida takes the railing hand over hand. There is no time to consider Kowalchuck, who Marcello believes may well be immortal, as he claimed. By the time they stagger out onto Canal Road, the candy store is a ball of fire, the flames fed by the Depression-era sawdust used to insulate the building's walls. Marcello can hear the sirens of fire trucks crossing the canal bridge.

Debris rains down on them. Bits of lath and scorched roof tiles float to earth like burnt leaves. Neighbours have left their TVs to gather on the street – the Hryhorchucks, Claudia Donato, Angela So-and-So, some of the craps players. When Marcello sinks to his knees at the bottom of the fire escape, Claudia runs to him with a shout, pulling the twins into her arms.

Marcello lays Pasquale on the ground, yanks his jeans up and looks into his face; his eyes are open but unfocused. *He's drunk*, Marcello realizes. Christie is beside him now, pulling a blanket around Ida. Marcello grabs Christie's arm: "Make sure the firemen take him to the hospital. Then you talk to Prima. Tell her I want her to make sure he's looked after. Someplace safe."

Christie nods. "Where are you going?

Marcello shakes his head. "I'll send you a message."

He leans down to kiss Pasquale, then entrusts him to Christie's care. Children looking after children seems to be the only hope.

In the Chevy, Marcello pulls Ida into his arms. Paint is sliding off her face in silver tears. She smells like sulfur and her mouth stings against his.

He holds her, and holds her, and wonders whether they should just stay here like this, growing old together, letting the world revolve around their everlasting embrace. Eventually he and Ida and the Chevy would transform into a garden or a stand of birch trees, like in a classical myth or one of those operas from the old country.

*Ridiculous,* he tells himself. This is Canada. We have to be practical.

With his arms still around Ida, he says, "The faster we get out of Niagara, the less chance they have of stopping us. I have enough money to get us anywhere you want to go. We'll be okay. Ready?"

Ida nods her head.

"*Avanti.* Just drive."

Marcello twists together the ignition wires again – red, blue, green. The engine screams in agony, the tips of his fingers sizzle, but the starter catches and the engine turns over.

They make their getaway in a shower of sparks.

# 13

CHRISTIE STANDS ON THE stoop in her school uniform, waiting for the mail. She can see the postman in the distance, working his way along Canal Road; the last two weeks she's met him at the door every morning before she leaves for school. He's grown used to the ritual.

"Anything for me?"

He always shakes his head. "Not yet, but don't worry. I'm keeping my eye out."

This time, though, he mounts the stairs to the stoop to hand her two pieces of mail: one of them a white legal envelope, the other, a postcard.

"Good luck," the postman says.

The legal envelope is postmarked *Guelph, Ontario*. This is it.

Christie doesn't open the letter right away. She watches the postman continue walking along Canal Road, past the old candy store. He never stops there anymore – the front stoop has finally collapsed, taking the mailbox with it. Anyway, who would send letters to a burned-out wreck? It's been up for sale for months. Rumour is that someone will buy the lot and put up a gas bar. Or maybe a Mac's Milk.

Finally, Christie takes a deep breath and opens the envelope.

It's a *yes*. She's been accepted: Arts and Sciences. She closes her eyes, letting the sun warm her face. In a moment, she'll go in and tell her mother. Telling her father will be more difficult. Not that there's anything he can do to stop her, really.

Pasquale will be sad. He'll miss her going out to the Andolini farm to tutor him but she'll find someone to keep up his reading. He's actually managed to get through most of *Do Androids Dream of Electric Sheep?* Not bad, for a twelve-year-old.

She looks at the postcard. A blonde rider on a black horse races around a barrel, leaning far to one side, waving her Stetson in the air. *Greetings from Prince George,* the words on the photograph say.

Flipping the postcard, she sees a one-line message, printed in a careful draughtsman's hand:

*Welcome to the World of Tomorrow.*
*Michael*

# ACKNOWLEDGEMENTS

My thanks go to the spirited team at Quattro Books for the Ken Klonsky Novella Award and the wisdom of editors of Luciano Iaccobelli and Allan Briesmaster. Thanks also to Maria Meindl, Heather McCulloch, Chris Caswell, Joey Edding, Jake Edding, Izzy Ferguson, Lynn Sproatt, Glen Petrie, Kris Rothstein, Guingo Sylwan, Annalisa Magnini-Sanangelantoni and Rick Favro for their advice and encouragement.

I wish to acknowledge *Accenti* magazine, where a section of *The Proxy Bride* was published in a slightly different form as the story, "Flora and Bruno." I am also grateful to Diaspora Dialogues for the mentorship of David Layton and publication of "A Shout from God", Marcello's 'origin' story, in *TOK Vol. 6*.

Finally, my deepest appreciation to my husband Ron and the Edding, Tessier, Hurd, Favro and Scrocchi families for the wine-and-memory-soaked meals, and for putting up with me.

# QUATTRO FICTION